ASHMORE UNIVERSITY FACULTY HANDBOOK

APPENDIX D

The purpose of granting tenure to faculty at Ashmore University is to ensure academic freedom and a reasonable expectation of continued employment following a rigorous review process. Tenure-track candidates must complete a probationary period of service as a full-time teaching member of our faculty, usually for a period of six to eight years before an official review process begins. Candidates will be evaluated on the basis of published scholarly research, teaching ability, grant procurement, and university service. Candidates will be evaluated by a majority of independent external reviewers not known to the candidate. The candidate's completed dossier will be reviewed and voted on only by tenured departmental faculty. Their recommendation along with the dossier will be forwarded to the University committee on Academic Promotion and Tenure for further review. The final recommendation by the APT committee will be forwarded to the Provost for a final decision by the University Board of Trustees.

TENURE

TO DIE FOR

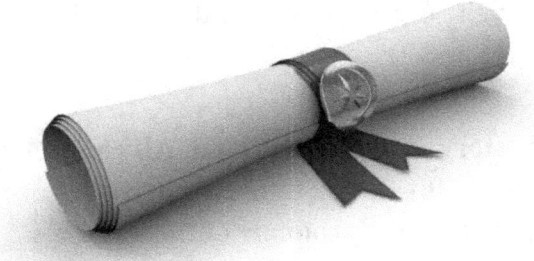

An Ivory Tower Murder Mystery

Ronald Perkins

ISBN: 978-0-578-15946-1

EXPLORIS PUBLISHING

Cover Painting by Salomon (de) Koninck (1609-
1656) entitled *The Old Scholar*

Chapters

CHAPTER 1: DEATH ON THE PARKWAY

As the small commuter plane descended through the clouds of western North Carolina, Alex Chandler grasped the armrests firmly as he stared out the window anxiously awaiting the first appearance of land. Barely perceptible at first, the runway of the small regional airport slowly emerged through the morning ground fog typical of the southern Appalachians, commonly referred to as the Smoky Mountains. The Bombardier CRJ-700, whipped by shifting gusts of wind, teetered back and forth until the pilot set it down gingerly on the runway, threw the thrusters in reverse, and taxied to the terminal. It was mid-October, and the heavily forested mountains encircling the airport were ablaze with brilliant colors of autumn leaves now at their peak. As Alex exited the plane he paused for a moment to savor the spectacular scenery and to inhale the fresh mountain air.

It was alumni reunion weekend at Ashmore University, a regional state campus nestled in the mountains of western North Carolina from which Alex had received his undergraduate degree in geology in 1963. Ashmore had been established as a land grant college in 1890 to serve the educational needs of rural communities in these western mountains. It was constructed on 4,000 acres deeded to North Carolina by the family of Joshua J. Ashmore, a Civil War soldier who survived the war and subsequently built a financial empire fueled by mining and forestry ventures. Ultimately, in the late 1940s, Ashmore College became Ashmore University as part of the state's multi-campus system. Over the ensuing years, the University grew not only in size, but also in academic stature, becoming one of the more highly regarded universities in the South. Highly qualified teachers and researchers were attracted to Ashmore, not only for its reputation, but also for its bucolic setting and for the way of life that it offered.

Alex retrieved his luggage at the baggage claim area and made his way to the car rental counter.

Rentals were at a premium owing to the seasonal invasion of tourists who had come for fall foliage colors and the delightful weather, as well as Ashmore alumni who were arriving a few days early for the reunion. Alex had reserved a mid-sized sedan over the Internet but was informed that none were available at the moment. However, he was offered the option of a large gas-guzzling SUV at no extra cost if he preferred not to wait on the outside chance that a mid-sized sedan might be returned later that day. Alex thought that there wasn't a snowball's chance in hell that that was going to happen and opted for the SUV. The trip he had planned would be especially enjoyable as most of the route from the airport to Ashmore would follow the Blue Ridge Parkway. He exited the small airport lobby and waited curbside for his SUV to be brought from the car rental's remote parking area.

At last the large black Chevy Tahoe arrived with all its bells and whistles. Still a bit miffed at his rental compromise, Alex loaded his luggage, boarded the behemoth, opened the sunroof and sped off. By the time he reached the interstate, Alex had calmed down and was beginning to adapt to, and even enjoy, the luxurious ride and view from his perch high above the passing cars. As it was Thursday, traffic along the parkway would not be as heavy as it would be on the upcoming weekend when swarms of tourists would gather to marvel at the annual kaleidoscope of fall colors before the trees shed their leaves and remain stark naked until their reawakening in the spring. The evergreens would provide some color in the winter, but they were mostly monochromatic and far less interesting.

After driving for a half-hour or so, Alex exited the interstate at signage indicating an entrance to the Blue Ridge Parkway and a visitor center a short distance away. Alex stopped at the center to pick up a parkway map and gather information concerning noteworthy sites along the way. As he entered the building, which was tastefully designed in a log cabin motif, his attention was drawn to a large photographic wall mural featuring a view of the parkway. An accompanying text described how President Franklin Roosevelt created the Parkway project in the 1930s as part of his New Deal. The parkway was designed to link the Shenandoah National Park in Virginia with the Smoky Mountains National Park in North Carolina. The project was finally completed in 1987 when the Linn Cove Viaduct was formally dedicated, thus creating a continuous 469 mile-long ribbon of asphalt that draws twenty million visitors annually.

The visitor center attendants were most cordial and offered to assist Alex in any way that they could. Alex was assured that the road was open despite the fact that recent heavy rains had produced washouts along the way where he might encounter a few short delays. Alex thanked them for their help and then spent a few minutes perusing the myriad of brochures filling the racks that lined the walls. He picked up a few flyers describing restaurants and accommodations near Ashmore. After all, it had been several years since he had returned to his alma mater, and he anticipated many changes.

Alex began his trip along the winding route, his eyes concealed by dark sunglasses. He soon became totally engrossed in scanning the road cuts and vistas for things of a geological nature. Shimmering outcrops of granite shot through with veins of white quartz glistened in the sun. The recent heavy rains had raised the local groundwater table giving rise to numerous springs that sent water cascading down the rocky slopes. As the center attendants had warned, a few small landslides created one-way traffic delays as parkway crews worked to clear the road. Even though it was a weekday, turnoffs and overlooks with far-reaching vistas were crowded with tourists feverishly snapping photos of the fall foliage, capturing hundreds of digital images of the same thing, and hoping for that one perfect scene that would be suitable for framing as a reminder of their excursion through the mountains.

For all its beauty, Alex was aware that the parkway was deceptively dangerous and that travelling along this narrow, two-lane road required that a driver remain vigilant. Drivers often encounter steep drop-offs descending hundreds of feet down mountain slopes without adequate guardrail protection. Blind curves bound by sheer rock faces on one side and narrow shoulders on the other challenge even the best of drivers. Dense fog can appear without warning, limiting visibility to a terrifying few tens of feet. Illegal passing by impatient drivers annoyed by the forty-five mph speed limit can leave oncoming traffic with no exit strategy. Aware that all these dangers were potential recipes for disaster, Alex continued on his way.

Alex slammed on his brakes when a tour bus that he had been following slowed down abruptly and pulled off the parkway in order to allow passengers to disembark and enjoy one of the most impressive views along the entire parkway— the Linn Cove Viaduct. Alex stopped to join them for he knew the viaduct had been recognized internationally as an engineering marvel. It was designed to minimize the environmental impact of road construction as it hugs the southern face of Grandfather Mountain, one of the most beloved landmarks in the southern Appalachians. After photo enthusiasts were satisfied that they had captured the perfect image, everyone began to board the bus. Alex maneuvered his SUV back onto the parkway ahead of the bus, weary of trailing the bus for so many miles, annoyed by its diesel fumes, and resenting the obstruction of his view. A few miles before the exit to Blowing Rock, Alex pulled to a stop behind a long line of cars confined to a single lane by a flagman halting traffic. After the south traveling traffic was allowed to pass, the flagman motioned for northbound traffic to continue. Traffic moved slowly down a steep grade that gave way to a hair-pin turn at its base. As Alex approached the curve he saw a work crew busy repairing a broken guardrail that was meant to shield the road from a sharp drop-off to the valley floor below. Alex knew that particular curve well from his days at Ashmore and remembered it as one of the most dangerous on the Parkway. The gaping hole in the wooden guardrail gave mute testimony to a horrific crash that likely claimed someone's life. Alex noticed that there were no skid marks leading up to the crash site. *Whoever crashed through that barrier must have been going like a bat out of hell,* thought Alex as he drove past the repair crew.

Two-way traffic soon resumed and before long Alex found himself entering the town of Blowing Rock. It was not as he had remembered. A large outlet mall featuring high-quality brands at discount prices caught his attention, as did the newer homes and refurbished older houses that clearly hinted at the affluence of its residents. Traffic was heavy as tourists milled around the numerous specialty shops and restaurants along the main street with weary shoppers occupying most of the benches in the city park across the street. Automobiles patiently crawled along the side streets in their futile quest for limited parking spaces.

Alex was relieved when he was finally able to escape the congestion in Blowing Rock and soon found himself driving on a less travelled road through the familiar surroundings of the town of Waltonville, home to his alma mater. His perception of the town was that it hadn't changed all that much since he left but had retained the small-town atmosphere that he treasured so much so many years before. Without much difficulty, Alex was able to navigate the familiar narrow streets of Waltonville until he arrived at the University Inn where he checked in and settled into his room.

Alex had arranged to meet one his former teaching colleagues, Dr. Chris Carpenter, who also would be attending the reunion and staying at the University Inn. As Chris wouldn't be arriving from Atlanta until tomorrow, Alex thought he would catch up with another of his old colleagues, Paul Armstrong, a civil engineering professor who at the age of seventy-five was still teaching at Ashmore. He and Paul served together on several university committees and, over time became good friends. They also collaborated on a few research papers when their scientific interests overlapped. Their families became close and they often attended university functions together.

Alex checked his cell phone for Paul's number and although it had been years since he had called him, thought it still might be a working number. After the phone rang three or four times Paul's wife answered.

"Hello, Alice. Alex Chandler here. Is Paul there?"

There was a long pause with no response.

"Oh, Alex, I thought you knew. I hate to give you the bad news, but Paul is dead."

"Paul is dead? That can't be. I spoke with him just last week about the class reunion."

"I'm sorry, but it's true. It was a horrible accident."

"What happened?"

"According to the officer who investigated the accident, Paul was driving his old Jaguar at a high rate of speed along the Blue Ridge Parkway when his brakes failed. He must have lost control and crashed through the barrier. The car rolled over and over down the ravine...."

Alice began sobbing uncontrollably. Alex now realized that the very signs of an accident he had just seen on the parkway were those that involved Paul.

"Alice, I'm so sorry. I didn't know. It's such a tragedy…. Such a loss."

It was several minutes before Alex could console Alice enough to continue the conversation.

"Is there anything that I can do for you? I'll be in town for the rest of the week for the reunion. I'm staying at the University Inn. Please let me know. Paul was a good friend and colleague. I'll miss him. Don't hesitate to call me."

"Thank you, Alex. I'll be alright. The kids were all here for the funeral and our daughter is staying with me for a few more days. I'll be fine."

After Alice hung up the phone, Alex sat there in silence, still reeling from the realization that Paul was dead. Paul was known as a meticulous researcher at Ashmore, but not highly regarded as a teacher. Alex knew that all of Paul's spare time was spent restoring the vintage XKE Jaguar that had claimed his life. He remembered how passionate Paul was about that car and how careful he was at keeping it maintained and in tip-top shape despite the fact that it was over fifty years old. Alex couldn't believe that Paul would allow something as serious as the car's brakes to be neglected. It just didn't fit. Something was wrong.

CHAPTER 2: RECOLLECTIONS

As it was mid-afternoon and a beautiful day, Alex decided to tour the campus that was only a short distance from the hotel. As he strolled along the campus pathways past familiar buildings, Alex began to reflect on his past experiences at Ashmore and how it came to pass that he became part of the institution itself. He recalled how he struggled as an undergraduate trying to find himself. Initially he thought he would major in mechanical engineering, but his first day in class changed all that. The professor led off his lecture with the time-worn admonition, "Look at the student in front of you, the one behind you, and those on each side. Only one of you will be here in four years." Alex transferred within the first week to the College of Arts and Sciences without a clue as to what he would choose as a major.

Everyone had to take a science elective as part of the A&S core curriculum, and Alex picked the introductory course in geology that he had heard wasn't as rigorous as chemistry or physics. The course was taught by a dynamic professor, Dr. Charles Alexander. To his surprise, Alex found the course more difficult than he had anticipated, but it piqued his interest. Soon he began to think seriously about geology as a major. After taking a few more courses and participating in several departmental field trips to study outcrops in the Appalachian Mountains, Alex was hooked and chose geology as his major field of study.

As an undergraduate, Alex was fully engaged in campus activities and belonged to several organizations. He was president of his fraternity, as well as president of the Inter-fraternity Council. He was a walk-on member of the school's basketball team, the Bobcats, but saw limited playing time as he topped out at only six feet one inch. He was elected class president in his senior year and named "Mr. Bobcat," an award given to a graduating senior who distinguished himself through university service and school spirit.

During his undergraduate days, Alex dated many of more popular co-eds on the campus, but as a senior settled down in a serious relationship with Pamela Morrison, a vivacious and beautiful cheerleader who was completing her degree in elementary education. Alex proposed to Pamela on New Year's Eve, and they planned a June wedding after graduation. During the spring semester of his senior year, Alex was offered and accepted a graduate teaching assistantship in geology at Yale University. After the wedding, the couple rented an apartment in Charlotte, North Carolina, near Pamela's parents. That summer Alex found employment as a field assistant on a U.S. Geological Survey mapping project and Pamela worked at a day-care center. In late August they loaded up their limited possessions into a U-Haul trailer and headed for New Haven, Connecticut.

In short order, Alex became totally engrossed in his graduate studies, while Pamela found a part-time job at a local bookstore. The possibility of a teaching position in elementary education that she had hoped for never materialized. As time passed, Pamela became more discontented with her role as a struggling housewife subsisting on Alex's meager stipend and her minimum-wage job. His studies were becoming all-consuming and left little time for Pamela who was becoming more resentful of their strained relationship. The straw that broke the camel's back came when Alex announced that he wanted to continue his studies beyond a master's degree and pursue a doctoral degree.   Two rocky years of marriage ended in a contentious divorce with Pamela receiving virtually nothing in the settlement.

Pamela left for Charlotte and moved in with her parents until she could find a teaching job and begin her life anew. Alex stayed on at Yale and after three more years of arduous work, received his PhD in geology with a specialty in the emerging field of geophysics.

Alex thought that eventually he would like to teach at the college level, but he felt that practical experience and a healthy industrial salary would be a better starting point for his career. He accepted a position with a major oil company's research lab in Houston, Texas, in August of 1972. Much of his time was spent field testing and evaluating sophisticated instrumentation that would aid the company in its oil exploration efforts. He was promoted rapidly up the corporate ladder and, after five years was named director of the company's research lab. His executive secretary, Victoria Wilson, a very attractive widow, became his confidant, his lover, and after a year, his second wife.

Five years later, he was transferred to head up the company's offshore exploration operations in the Gulf of Mexico. Alex and Victoria now had two small children that they adored, Allison and Alisha. While he found the managerial position he held satisfying financially and scientifically, he had this gnawing feeling in his gut that something was missing in his life. The demands of his job with its attendant administrative responsibilities seemed to consume all of his time and energy. He began to question whether or not he was cut out for a lifelong career in industry. There was always a risk when companies hired PhDs that they might eventually become disenchanted with industry and long to return to academia. After much soul-searching, Alex realized that he missed the reawakening that occurred every fall on university campuses when the new academic year began, fueled by promising new students and challenges in esoteric research. But his longings were tempered by the significant cut in pay he would have to endure if he were to make such a change in his career. Besides, opportunities to teach at quality universities were few and far between. Reluctantly, Alex became resigned to the fact that such a prospect would have to be put on hold.

Then unexpectedly, Alex was invited to give a departmental seminar at Ashmore as part of the department's distinguished alumni series. Despite the secretive nature of his industrial position, company permission had been granted Alex to present results of his earlier research efforts at professional meetings, after they were no longer considered to be of strategic value to the company. Such releases were fairly common in other oil company research labs as well, because they added to the stature and reputation of the companies that they represented. Alex presented one of his professional meeting talks that had been cleared by his company a few months earlier. His seminar was first class, not only the content, but also with respect to the graphic illustrations that had been prepared by his company's audio-visual department.

At a reception held in his honor following the presentation, Alex was cornered by the departmental chairman and asked if he had any interest in a new faculty position that was going to open at Ashmore in his field of expertise. Unlike today, no extensive search was required then before hiring new faculty, and Alex was offered the job by the Dean of the Faculty within a week after returning to Houston.

Over the next week, Alex and Victoria weighed the pros and cons of leaving industry for academia. On the positive side, Houston was a progressive, bustling city with fine restaurants, major sporting events, a symphony orchestra, a host of cultural attractions, superb medical facilities, fine shopping, and affordable housing. There were also the many friendships they had forged at work and in their suburban Woodlands neighborhood. On the negative side, Houston was still growing at an alarming rate, and traffic had become a major problem for any commuter. An hour each way to and from work was not unusual. Heat and high humidity were at times unbearable and greatly restricted outdoor activity in the summer. With the exception of bone-chilling rainy days, the winters generally were tolerable.

On the other hand, Ashmore University was located in Waltonville, a charming mountain town in in western North Carolina, favored by tourists in the summer for its pleasant climate, the fall for its spectacular scenery with bursts of color from the changing foliage, and in the winter for its relatively mild climate with enough snow to provide skiing at the nearby slopes. The possibility of a short drive to work was an appealing aspect, as well as the fact that the drive would be on a forested, winding mountain road rather than a high-speed freeway. Another important consideration in their decision was the opportunity for their children to attend the highly regarded University School associated with Ashmore University. The prospect of raising their children in a small-town environment was also of paramount importance.

Despite the disparity in salary, Alex accepted the offer from Ashmore, sold their suburban home in Houston in short order and purchased a smaller, but comfortable, mountain log home located a few miles outside of Waltonville, surrounded by lush thickets of rhododendron and mountain laurel.

The fact that Alex already had several publications to his credit allowed him to negotiate an initial appointment as an associate professor without tenure. Previous publications aside, tenure was a major decision that would not be considered until Alex had a proven record of teaching and additional peer-reviewed publications while at Ashmore. Alex quickly adapted to his new position and soon became one of the department's most popular professors. His courses were almost always wait-listed.

Alex looked the part of the distinguished college professor. In the vernacular of the day, his attire was referred to as preppy. In the cooler weather he wore tasteful Harris tweeds or corduroy jackets with leather patches on the elbows. In the warmer months he wore a tasteful blue blazer, collar open with no tie, and Sperry-Topsiders. Age had spared his hair, which now had streaks of gray and was closely-cropped. Alex resisted the urge to grow a beard in deference to Victoria's wishes, and was clean-shaven. No tattoos adorned his arms or any other part of his body. During his entire teaching career he was so attired, not yielding to the jeans and T-shirt craze championed by the newer faculty hires.

After a career spanning thirty years, having achieved the rank of full professor at the age of forty, and with numerous academic accolades along the way, Alex relinquished tenure at age sixty-five and was granted professor emeritus status. He sold his Waltonville Mountain retreat for a handsome profit and retired to Hilton Head Island on the South Carolina coast. In retirement, Alex was able to establish a lucrative consulting business, drawing on contacts with his former students who now held prominent positions in the oil industry. He now could work as much or as little as he wished and could spend as much time as he liked with his wife, children, and now, four grandchildren. He also had ample time to devote to his life-long passion for golf with twenty courses located in Hilton Head or nearby in the low country. Alex became an avid salt-water fisherman and an active member of the Hilton Head Audubon Society. He especially enjoyed the explosive bird migrations that occurred every spring, as well as the flocks of southward migrating birds in the fall. Although he could have elected to teach at Ashmore for many more years, he never once regretted his decision to retire. Alex was a happy and contented man.

Returning to campus for the reunion that embraced all the graduating classes from 1960 through 1970 was a bittersweet experience for Alex. He reminisced about the constant pressure that he had endured to secure funding for his research and student support, and all those years of struggling to prove himself worthy of tenure. Then there were always the petty departmental politics to contend with.   These recollections were tempered by his "bright spots", an endearing term he used to refer to his most-gifted students. It was only after each received his or her doctoral degree that Alex told them that they could stop addressing him as Dr. Chandler and could now address him simply as Alex. It was a well-established tradition that every one of his students looked forward to.

Alex continued his walk across campus, unable to get the devastating news of Paul's untimely death out of his mind. Lost in his thoughts, Alex soon found himself at the arched stone entrance to the Ashmore Campus on University Drive within sight of his hotel. He returned to his room, showered and decided to have an early supper. After dining alone in the hotel restaurant, Alex retired to his room, fired up his laptop, and began to search the local newspaper's online archives for information concerning Paul's accident. The story line was that it had been a tragic accident with faulty brakes being blamed for the crash. High speed was suspected, but there were no witnesses to the accident. As a matter of fact, Paul's car was not discovered until the next day. Had someone been able to reach Paul sooner, perhaps his life could have been saved.

I think we need to have a look at that car, thought Alex. *I'm sure Chris will be as skeptical about this accident as I am.*

After Alex perused the innumerable emails that had accumulated over the past two days, deleting most of them as being purely superfluous, he turned off the laptop and settled into his bed to watch the national news and found it to be as depressing as always. He turned off the TV and reached for a novel that he had been reading. After an hour or so, he dozed off and slept until being roused by the hotel wake-up call at seven o'clock in the morning.

CHAPTER 3: STUDENT ANGST

Alex picked up the paper that had been placed outside his door and made his way to the hotel dining room, where he was treated to a country buffet breakfast consisting of eggs, fried ham, homemade biscuits, locally-preserved blackberry jam, and grits. He hadn't had grits since he left Ashmore decades ago and thoroughly enjoyed getting reacquainted with the regional dish. After downing a few cups of coffee and reading the local paper, Alex returned to his room, grabbed a fleece jacket, and exited the hotel into a crisp fall day with wind gusts that brought a bit of chill to the air. He felt invigorated as fresh mountain air filled his lungs, and his steps quickened as he walked towards the building where he had taught so many years before.

Alex caught the exodus from the surrounding buildings as classes were dismissed. He was struck by the change in demographics as the students walked between classes. The student population clearly had become multinational. He noted that many of the students, especially the women, were dressed in the latest fashions. Leather jackets, high-topped boots, colorful scarves, cashmere sweaters, and designer jeans were now the status symbols for those who could afford the wardrobe. For the men, with only a few exceptions, not much had changed. Jeans, khaki pants, sweatshirts, sneakers, and down vests or jackets were the order of the day. Ubiquitous backpacks, some grossly overloaded, were draped over most of the students' backs. For some unknown reason, most of the packs sported the "North Face" logo.

Everywhere Alex looked it seemed that someone was either talking on a cell phone, listening to music on their iPod, or sitting on the lawn browsing the Internet with their iPad or laptop. Walking past conversing students one couldn't help but notice the diversity of languages that were being spoken.   Alex wondered what had driven the diversity. Was it a natural evolution of an ever-changing world, or could it have been driven by tuition-based economics? It was likely that the international students were paying full tuition costs without any financial aid provided. Perhaps it was a combination of the two.

Alex arrived at the geology building and observed that it hadn't changed much except for the signage out front indicating that the building was now called the Franklin School of Earth Sciences. It appeared that Ashmore finally had been able to secure a sizable donation in exchange for a naming opportunity. The facade of the limestone-faced building had been sandblasted and given a much-needed facelift. Upon entering the building, Alex was struck by the new tile flooring and the fresh coat of paint on the walls that were adorned with colorful posters of presentations by the faculty and students at professional meetings. He wandered down the hall until he reached the room that had served as the student lounge during his tenure at Ashmore. He was pleased to find it intact and occupied by two students who were sitting at the table drinking coffee. Alex introduced himself, grabbed a cup of coffee, and asked if he could join them.

"Of course. Delighted to have you join us Dr. Chandler. I recognize your name. I know you were on the faculty here some time ago, and I'm familiar with some of the papers that you published. My dissertation is focusing on an area in the Pisgah National Forest not too far from the area you mapped back in the'80s. I'm Tyler Ryan, and this is Jeremy Waters."

"Good to meet you both. How close are you guys to graduating?"

"I hope to be graduating next June," said Tyler.

"I've got two more years before I get my PhD. That is, if I'm lucky and don't run out of money before then," said Jeremy.

"Aren't you guys on financial aid?"

"Yes, but it's difficult to make ends meet on the stipend alone, especially if you're married. My wife works at a local gift shop to help make ends meet. The problem is that I began graduate school four years ago saddled with a student loan debt of $50,000 that I still owe. In addition, my wife's parents have loaned us an additional $20,000 just to keep us afloat."

Hearing this, Alex was reminded of how fortunate he was when he graduated. At that time, tuition costs were considerably lower. He was on a full scholarship while in graduate school and was always employed during the summers. He had no student loan debt and actually had money in the bank after graduation.

"What do you plan to do after graduation, Tyler?" asked Alex.

"I always planned to teach, but I don't know if that is even a possibility in today's tight job market. And then there is the fact that a PhD degree alone just isn't enough. All of us are looking into post-doc positions after graduation to strengthen our publication record and to bide our time until positions open in our fields. A post-doc seems to be a necessity nowadays to even be considered for a good teaching position. A nine-year college stint to get a PhD only to be followed by two or more years in a post-doc position with no guarantee of a job in sight can be disheartening and a bit frustrating to say the least. Part of the problem is that faculty aren't retiring at age sixty-five as they used to in the old days. We have good old Senator Claude Pepper to thank for the bill abolishing age discrimination in employment and ending mandatory retirement."

Alex replied, "Someday, Tyler, when you're old and gray, perhaps you'll appreciate what Pepper did for all of us. He fought for the elderly, the poor, and the disenfranchised. He believed that government had a responsibility to care for all of its citizens by ensuring that they had equal opportunity, health care, and personal security. He was a great public servant. But I see how the unintended consequence of his bill affects your present situation."

Alex continued, "How about you, Jeremy? What are your plans for the future? "

"I'm keeping my options open. I used to be anti-industry, but in my field the only really good opportunities seem to be in the oil business. Didn't you work in industry before you began teaching?"

"Yes, for about ten years. I learned as much in industry as I ever did in graduate school because everything was driven by applied science and the bottom line. Unlike many arm-waving scientists with theories that can be neither proven nor disproven, your reasoning is going to be confirmed or denied by the drill bit. Someone is going to put money on the line, perhaps millions of dollars, and your conclusions are going to be tested. You hope your recommendation is an economic success, not just a geologic success. But you don't get fired for drilling a dry hole. We learn from our mistakes. Your job is to create more opportunities for your company. It's back to the drawing board for a new idea or a new approach, and that can be very challenging and stimulating. Don't give up on industry, Jeremy. It can be very fulfilling and a great way to make a living."

"Thanks for the encouragement. Unfortunately I might not even have a choice between teaching and industry with the scarcity of teaching jobs available. I just feel fortunate to be in a field where other types of job opportunities exist. I have a lot of friends working on PhDs in fields with little hope of finding any kind of employment in their chosen specialties. Academic positions in the humanities are hard to come by and very competitive. Let me show you what I mean."

Jeremy took his iPad out of his backpack and typed in a website he had discovered that listed available jobs for PhDs.

"You can search for jobs for PhDs by fields such as life sciences, humanities, or social sciences, by sectors such as academia, industry, or government openings, by job type such as tenure or non-tenure track faculty or research positions, or by searching selected geographic localities. Here, let me show you," said Jeremy sharing his iPad with Alex.

"This year there are approximately ten thousand jobs available in all categories in four-year institutions. Actually, this is a big improvement over last year when there were only about nine thousand openings. I don't know why the number jumped up so dramatically this past year, but I hope it's a trend. On the downside, do you know how many PhDs were awarded last year?   Almost fifty thousand! Fewer than one out of five had a chance of landing a job! I think you can see what we're up against.

"Some are saying that the whole PhD situation is getting out of hand and have levied strong criticism of the system in the United States. I read an article recently that characterized PhD students as being educated and trained too narrowly, taking too long to complete doctoral studies, lacking organizational and managerial skills including teamwork, and being poorly prepared to teach and ill-informed about non-academic employment.

"It may well be that we are trained too narrowly, but demonstrating expertise in some specialized field and being recognized by your peers in that field often weigh heavily in tenure decisions. We had a faculty member here last year who was denied tenure because he was too broad in his interests. You get the distinct impression that being a generalist just won't cut it when it comes to tenure.

"I don't know if you are aware of the increasing role that contingent faculty are playing in academia. Universities are relying heavily on transient faculty, often referred to as "road scholars", because many of them teach at more than one university. According to a recent survey more than half of US college instructors are adjuncts, part-time teachers, TAs, or untenured professors.

"And then there is the new trend toward online courses. Several universities have courses that they offer to fewer than one hundred students in the classroom and close to ninety thousand others online. What we may have in the future is a "superstar" lecturer supported by non-tenured PhDs acting as glorified teaching assistants who monitor the lecture and handle all the questions from those online. Also, they would likely monitor tests and be responsible for assigning grades if these courses receive credit. It could be that we never have an opportunity to perform a traditional teaching role. As the Bob Dylan song goes, 'the times they are a-changin'.'"

Jeremy continued, "There is however, a ray of hope on the job horizon. Terry Roberts, one of our doctoral students who graduated last spring, was able to secure a teaching job at A&M through a new employment agency called Academic Appointment Placement Services, or AAPS. You provide them with your academic background information, your minimum salary requirement, your area of expertise, and what courses in your field you would feel capable of teaching. You indicate your preference for either a large state or private university with a strong graduate program or a small liberal arts college with an emphasis on undergraduate education. You may consider a community college, a technical school, or even a private secondary school. AAPS charges an upfront fee to initiate a search for you to the tune of $5,000, and if they are not successful in finding you a position within a year, they will refund the money. If they do find you a position, you will be obligated to pay them an additional fee equivalent to one month's salary at the end of your first academic year."

"Sounds like a scam to me," said Alex. "Aren't all the available academic positions advertised nationally anyway?"

"AAPS claims that it has the most extensive academic database available. They monitor faculty retirements, deaths, and new appointment authorizations before the information gets distributed widely. I don't know if there is anything going on under the table to acquire this information, but it surely worked for Terry. When he was advised by AAPS of the untimely death of one of the faculty in his field at A&M, Terry visited the department, introduced himself to many of the faculty, and offered to give an informal seminar highlighting his cutting-edge research. They were impressed with his initiative and his resumé and the deal was effectively sealed even though the position was advertised nationally a few weeks later as the department went through the requisite steps to meet the spirit of the required national search."

Alex finished his coffee, thanked Tyler and Jeremy for their insights, and headed back to his hotel to spend some time on the Internet searching for answers to many nagging questions. The revelation that such a company as AAPS existed was disturbing to him and suggested that it was possible that this was an unethical company preying on desperate graduate students seeking academic jobs. What would become of the students who couldn't afford to hire such an agency with the hope of securing a job? Wouldn't they be at an unfair disadvantage when competing for jobs?

Alex wondered about the consequences of universities producing PhDs in numbers that the job market can't accommodate. Is there a moral obligation on the part of universities to somehow let students know up front what to expect upon graduation? Should potential employment opportunities even be a topic of discussion on university campuses? For Tyler and Jeremy, are they just victims of poor timing as the pendulum for job opportunities has historically swung back and forth from feast to famine, reflecting the overall health of the economy? Are many graduate students trapped in a holding pattern until the job market improves? How long will they have to wait?

CHAPTER 4: RESEARCH AND REFLECTION

After dinner, Alex returned to his hotel room and began to browse the Internet. He was particularly interested in what the criteria were nowadays for academic promotion and tenure. It was remarkably easy to find information for most universities. He spent considerable time reviewing the academic freedom and tenure polices of several universities and was struck by how similar they were. Academic freedom was clearly stated up front as the right to discover, speak, and teach the truth. The university would encourage that freedom and protect all faculty members in the exercise of these freedoms against influences that would restrict his or her area of scholarly discourse. Matters outside the areas of scholarly interests would not be protected by the university, but by the same freedoms enjoyed by citizens in general. No faculty member could represent himself or herself as a spokesman for the university unless authorized by the university to do so.

With regard to tenure, Alex observed how much more rigorous the requirements seemed to be than those required when he was granted tenure at Ashmore many years before. In addition to a detailed curriculum vita, other requirements typically included: a synopsis of intellectual interests, a statement summarizing research, outlines of courses taught, teaching evaluations, university service, a list of supervised theses and dissertations, a list of the candidate's most significant publications, a list of collaborators on publications, grants recently awarded and those pending, copies of published reviews of the candidate's papers, and a minimum of six external letters from reviewers who have no connection to the candidate. These documents would be screened and reviewed at several administrative levels and ultimately presented before the academic promotion and tenure committee for advancement or denial of tenure. The entire process might take six months to a year before any official action would be taken.

It was clear to Alex that at research institutions, tenure would be awarded on the basis of published research results, professional recognition by peers in the candidate's field, and on the successful procurement of grants to support further research and graduate student stipends. Overhead and indirect costs embedded in such research grants constitute an important part of funding a first-class research institution. The ability to teach is considered a given, and although teaching is considered in evaluating a candidate, tenure is not awarded on the basis of teaching alone at most, if not all, research institutions. In contrast, at smaller liberal arts colleges teaching ability is generally regarded as having a higher priority in the granting of tenure.

Alex knew the tenure decision to be an issue of great importance to both the candidate being proposed for tenure as well as to the university whose reputation is based on the quality and prominence of its faculty. Granting tenure represents a long-term commitment on the part of the university with the candidate and assures him or her that employment is guaranteed until such time as he or she decides to retire. Tenured faculty can be dismissed as a result of egregious or unseemly behavior, breaking the law, incompetence, neglect of duty, violations of professional ethics, or dissolution of the department or school with which the faculty member is affiliated. While it was hoped that granting of tenure would be a prelude to continued growth and professional development of associate professors aspiring to become full professors, that wasn't always the case. Alex knew of instances where faculty abused their tenured status. In one case in the physics department, an assistant professor who was an agreeable colleague before tenure became a proverbial "pain in the ass" as soon as tenure was granted. He was belligerent at faculty meetings, let his courses slide, and seemed content to "coast into retirement." He couldn't care less whether or not he would ever become a full professor. He was clearly a liability, not an asset, and everyone was greatly relieved when he resigned and assumed a position at another university. However, he was clearly the exception, not the rule.

For the individual who is being considered for tenure, a negative vote can be devastating. In addition to having been an undergraduate student for four years, a graduate student for four or five years, followed in many cases by a year or two as a post-doc, a tenure track candidate typically spends at least four more years as an assistant professor before even being considered for promotion to associate professor with tenure. It is rare for any faculty member denied tenure to be allowed to stay on at the university in some capacity, and it basically is a "get out of town" card. There have been instances where such decisions may have resulted in a candidate's suicide or retaliation against faculty members or administrators who voted in favor of denying tenure. For many the stigma of a failed career in academia is something they may carry for a lifetime.

Others who have been denied tenure may be more fortunate. Alex knew that a few prestigious universities may deny tenure to its assistant professors as a matter of course. Other universities, aware of this practice, often hire these "rejects," many of them become outstanding scholars and tenured professors at their new institutions. Others find jobs at smaller liberal arts colleges, regional state campuses, community colleges, or leave academia permanently to pursue opportunities in industry, government, or business where a PhD is highly valued. For some it may mean accepting a job for which they are significantly overqualified.

Alex was aware that numerous blogs and op-ed pages have created the perception among the general public that tenured university professors teach only a few hours a week, work only nine months a year with breaks in the fall, at Thanksgiving, at Christmas, between semesters, and in the spring. Faculty are periodically entitled to sabbatical leave, a semester off with full pay. They often relegate the grading of exams to graduate students, and publish research on esoteric subjects with little or no practical application and, to top it off, they have been guaranteed jobs for life.   Against a backdrop of constantly rising tuition costs and highly publicized salaries of university administrators, there is little wonder that there is some resentment by those in the general population, especially by those who are unemployed.

While there is a grain of truth in this criticism, Alex knew that these generalizations were misleading and exaggerated. Based on his own experience, Alex found that most faculty members in his department worked forty hours or more per week in preparing for classes, conducting active research, writing research papers for publication, preparing grant proposals, advising students, and serving on university committees. Summers were spent conducting research in the library, laboratory, or in the field. It should also be remembered that in order to get tenured positions, nine or more years of sacrifice were necessary to get hired in the first place, and further promotion would be determined by future research. While some of the research conducted by university faculty would immediately have practical application, the broader goal of increasing knowledge in general was also the charge of academia. One never knew if that which was considered esoteric today, would be applicable and important to society tomorrow. The perception that once tenure is granted, it is clear sailing for a professor is patently false. Faculty can't do as they damn well please as every faculty member's performance is scrutinized annually by the departmental chairman and reported to the dean. While a faculty member's poor performance in teaching or failing to secure grant support might not result in dismissal because she or he is tenured, there is always the threat of a heavier teaching load and no salary increase for that year. Conversely, those with considerable grant support involving many graduate students might be rewarded with a lighter teaching load and a significant increase in salary.

Alex shut down his laptop and sat there for a moment reflecting on his discussion with Tyler and

Jeremy. Clearly, job opportunities would be limited for them and far more competitive than they were in the past. Non-tenure track jobs with limited contracts likely would be much more common as universities were being squeezed financially by overhead and operational costs, and burdened by an aging, tenured faculty with higher salary commitments than those for new hires. Alex wondered how long the tenure-track system could survive. Would academic freedom survive without tenure or were they inexorably linked?   Had tenure outlived its relevance in academia? Was tenure stifling institutional progress? Should anyone be assured of permanent employment without a periodic review of performance? Alex had only to look at the terms of his prior employment in industry where performance was paramount and there were no guarantees of job longevity. Perhaps the time has come for tenure reevaluation.

CHAPTER 5: SUSPICIONS AROUSED

Alex awoke the next morning, had a leisurely breakfast, and then settled into a comfortable chair in the hotel lobby to read the *Wall Street Journal* as he awaited the arrival of his former colleague, Chris Carpenter, who was driving to Ashmore from his home in Augusta, Georgia. Assuming there were no travel snarls along the way, Chris was scheduled to meet Alex at the hotel at mid-morning. While he waited for Chris's arrival, Alex decided to call his wife and tell her of Paul's untimely death. Victoria was shocked to learn that Paul had died in an apparent accident and asked how Alice was holding up. He assured her that she seemed to be handling the unfortunate circumstances very well and that she had the support of her daughter, who had stayed behind to help her settle some of the estate affairs.

"I still think I'll call Alice to express my sorrow and offer to help her in any way that I can.

She was a good friend, and I can't imagine how she's going to get along without Paul. They were so good together."

"That would be very thoughtful, Victoria. I know she'd appreciate a call from you during this difficult time. I didn't want to alarm her, but I'm not convinced that this was an accident. After Chris arrives, I plan to go out and examine the wreckage to see if there's anything that seems suspicious. Whatever you do, Victoria, please don't give Alice any indication that I have any concerns about the cause of Paul's death. Honey, I see that Chris has just arrived here at the hotel. I need to go to the desk to meet him. I'll stay in touch. Give the kids a hug and a kiss for me. I'll see you in a few days. Love you. Bye-bye."

"Chris, it's so good to see you again!" said Alex, extending his hand in friendship. "It's been too long."

"Indeed it has, my friend. How have you been? And how is that lovely wife of yours?"

"I'm doing fine, but Victoria is keeping me on a short leash. I have a tendency to overextend myself on consulting jobs. I need her to keep me in check.

She's the counterbalance in my life, solid as a rock. How about you, and how's Marylyn doing? "

"She's as feisty as ever! She sends you her regards and told me to ask you to keep me out of trouble while we're here for the reunion," laughed Chris, fully intending to have a good time while he was here at Ashmore with his good friend. Alex knew that Chris was a recovering alcoholic and that it would be his responsibility to see that he didn't slip off the wagon under his watch.

"Let's get you checked in and then have lunch on campus."

Chris Carpenter had also received his undergraduate degree at Ashmore followed by graduate work at Scripps Institute of Oceanography, where he received his doctoral degree. Chris initially worked at Woods Hole Oceanographic Institute as a research scientist conducting studies on deep-sea hydrothermal vents, funded largely by government grants. During a period in which government grants were drastically reduced, Chris was recruited and hired by Ashmore, having been enticed by the promise of a steady job and weary of relying on soft money. Chris established himself as a highly respected scientist and teacher of marine science at Ashmore. He was considered an expert on coastal beach processes and authored several books on the subject. He retired at age sixty-five and with Marylyn, his wife of forty years, chose to live in Augusta, Georgia, to be near his daughter and their three grandchildren. Besides, he was also a longtime, die-hard Atlanta Braves fan.

Chris was ten years older than Alex and had been his mentor at Ashmore, shepherding him through the tenure review process while avoiding all the pitfalls along the way. They were also good fishing buddies who enjoyed fly fishing for native trout in the nearby mountain streams and hunting deer and wild turkeys in the fall. Alex found it somewhat ironic that Chris, a marine coastal geologist, chose to retire in land-locked Augusta, while he, a land-based geologist for his entire career, retired to the South Carolina coast.

While Chris was taking his bags to his room, Alex picked up a copy of the local newspaper to read until Chris returned. As chance would have it, Alex's eye caught a photo on the obituary page of a woman who looked vaguely familiar. As he read the obituary, he realized that it was Susan Sullivan, a professor of zoology, who had died at the age of 79. She was still teaching at Ashmore at the time of her death, which was ruled an accidental drowning. He recalled how he had served on a few university committees with Susan and had found her to be difficult to deal with. She was the first woman faculty hired by the zoology department and championed the cause of women faculty throughout her career, sometimes in a most abrasive manner. She was a strong advocate of women in science, a group she felt was under-represented on the faculty. In the classroom she was regarded as favoring women students over men and several formal protests were filed, but none ever resulted in a reprimand. Needless to say, Professor Sullivan never won any teaching awards. Nevertheless, two faculty deaths within a few weeks seemed unusual. Was it simply happenstance, or was there more to these "accidents"?

After Chris appeared in the lobby, Alex showed him the obituary page and asked if he had known Professor Sullivan while he was at Ashmore. He said that she looked vaguely familiar, but he wasn't sure he ever had any contact with her.

"I'm afraid I've got some other bad news for you, Chris. You remember my old friend, Paul Armstrong, in civil engineering? Unfortunately, he died in an automobile accident just last week on the Blue Ridge Parkway. At least they're calling it an accident."

"Why do you say that?"

"You remember how meticulous Paul was with that old Jaguar. The police said that his brakes failed. Paul was too good a mechanic to ever neglect his brakes. I'm not convinced that this was an accident. What do you say we check out the wreck and at least satisfy ourselves that there was nothing fishy going on? The wrecked car is being stored at Alpine Auto Salvage out on Highway 421. "

"Whatever you say, but it seems unlikely to me that such a thing would be anything other than an accident. But for now, I'm starving. Let's have some lunch."

The two left the hotel and began their walk across campus toward the Union Building that housed the Faculty Dining Room.

"I spent some time chatting with two graduate students in the geology department yesterday, and I can tell that today's doctoral students are in a hell of a fix. They are being squeezed by more financial burdens and fewer job opportunities than either of us ever had to deal with. We were damn lucky to have come along when we did."

As they walked, their conversation focused primarily on their families and how each had been spending his time in retirement. Chris was surprised at how successful Alex was with his consulting business and wished that he had an opportunity to do so as well. Chris was spending most of his time in his woodworking shop and busying himself with projects around their house. He wished that he too could supplement his retirement income with a few consulting jobs as his retirement cash flow had not quite lived up to his expectations. Consulting opportunities in marine geology were few and far between. He chose not to disclose his financial troubles to Alex.

CHAPTER 6: THE RETIREMEN CONUNDRUM

As they approached the Union Building, Alex noticed that something was missing. The beautiful *Gingko biloba* tree with its distinctive leaves that turned to brilliant yellow every fall was gone. Only a stump remained to mark its former presence.

"I loved that tree," said Alex. "I used to bring students over here every fall to show them this 'living fossil' with its leaves that are remarkably similar to fossil leaves that date back 270 million years. What a loss. It was a real landmark. A damn shame!"

They climbed the stairs to the second floor and entered the faculty dining room. It had the same furniture and ambiance they remembered from their past days at Ashmore. They were pleased to see that the large, round "Commons Table" in the center of the room remained. There were four faculty members seated at the table as Alex and Chris approached and asked if they could join them.

"Please do. Delighted to have you join us," responded a white-haired gentleman who stood up and extended his hand. Alex recognized him as Parker Johnson, a professor in the physics department. Alex was surprised that he was still teaching. Perhaps he had retired and he was just attending the reunion. Others seated at the table included Terry Swanson, a recently hired assistant professor in biomedical engineering, Frederick Underwood, a tenured professor in the religion department, and Allison Dubois, a tenured associate professor in romance languages. After the exchange of a few pleasantries, largely concerning the beautiful weather and the fall colors on campus, Alex asked about the recent death of Susan Sullivan and learned that she had died of an accidental drowning in her bathtub after suffering an apparent heart attack.

"Her death was a real shock to all of us," volunteered Parker, "as well as was the untimely death of Paul Armstrong in that unfortunate automobile accident. You know, Alex, we actually lost another faculty member this past summer,

Michael Emerson, who held an endowed chair in biomedical engineering. Perhaps you knew him. Michael drowned in a sail boating accident on Fontana Lake. He was apparently sailing by himself as was his custom. It was several days before they found his body. They discovered a large contusion on his head, which they attributed to being struck by the boom when the wind gusted unexpectedly. I actually had the opportunity to sail with Michael on more than one occasion, and frankly, I found the accident interpretation suspect. Michael was a first-class sailor, and I can't believe that he couldn't respond to an unexpected gust of wind. They felt that his age may have been a contributing factor as he was seventy-eight, but he was in better shape than many people I know who are half his age. The loss of three senior faculty members in less than a year has been a devastating loss for Ashmore.

"On the bright side, the school of engineering was able to replace Michael with an outstanding young assistant professor from MIT. He's already highly regarded and making a name for himself, even in such a short period of time. I assume that they will replace both Paul and Susan with similar junior faculty positions. After all we are still very heavily over-weighted with tenured senior faculty drawing considerably higher salaries."

"Parker, how long have you taught at Ashmore?" asked Alex.

"Fifty years and going strong. I celebrated my eightieth birthday last week. I think I am the oldest active faculty member on campus!"

"I'm curious, Parker, why you haven't retired after all these years."

"Frankly, I don't know what I would do with myself. I lost my wife, Marie, ten years ago. We had planned to retire when I was seventy and move to Toronto, Canada, to be near her family. Unfortunately, she succumbed to breast cancer after a most courageous battle with the disease. I had served as chairman of the physics department for ten years prior to her death. When I stepped down as chairman after her death, I found that my time away from research had left me outdated and non-competitive in the grant-securing game. But, I still could teach an introductory course in physics, and that is all I teach now. With the salary that they are paying me, I know that it is not in the best interest of the department and is a bit selfish on my part, but I think that if I didn't teach, I would die. It's not just about the money. Between my retirement savings and social security I could live very comfortably. You know they say now that staying employed and active helps delay the onset of Alzheimer's if you are predisposed to such a disease. It's just that if I have my way, I'll die clutching my notes at the podium," and he laughed heartily.   Alex couldn't help but recall Charlton Heston's famous NRA declaration, "I'll give you my gun when you pry it from my cold, dead hands."

Parker paused briefly… "How old were you when you retired, Alex?"

"I was sixty-five."

"Why did you retire?"

"After thirty years of teaching, I found that it just wasn't fun anymore. Besides, I wanted a change in my life and saw an opportunity to set up a consulting business and stay active in the energy industry. After seeing what happened to other faculty members who retired to play golf and fish without a plan to do anything else … well, let's just say I know three who died within two years after retiring."

"How about you, Chris, when did you retire?" continued Parker.

"I was sixty-five also. I was having some health issues that were interfering with my ability to do my job effectively."

Chris didn't disclose that his health issues had to do with alcohol abuse and some embarrassing classroom episodes that the university kept under wraps. It was strongly suggested that he retire rather than face dismissal for his behavior. Chris continued, "I have kept myself busy compiling historical accounts of tropical hurricanes and their impact on coastal communities along the eastern seaboard of the United States as well as the Caribbean Islands. It is actually quite a fascinating story that I hope will form the basis for a book I hope to publish on the subject."

Alex asked Frederick, the tenured professor in the religion department, at what age did he think he would retire.

"I just turned fifty this year, and I'm not sure I'd be able to retire at sixty-five even if I wanted to. As has been said, my 401K turned into a 201K after the last downturn in the market. You older guys were lucky. During the 1970s, '80s, and '90s, your retirement accounts had growth rates as much as 20 or 30 percent in some years. When you add in compounding, I bet both you guys are millionaires! I'll be damn lucky if I retire with half what you guys have. How do you think the market is going to perform in the next twenty years before I reach sixty-five? "

Alex and Chris were taken a bit aback and didn't know quite how to respond. They knew they were both lucky beneficiaries of the market's strong run during their tenure at Ashmore, and neither held out any hope that the market would ever perform again at that level before Frederick's retirement.

"You make a good point. I admit we were very lucky, but perhaps the market will see yet another run before you retire. I guess all we can do is hope that things get better, but I have to admit that our country's deficit spending practices, coupled with financial instability in the Euro-countries as well as unrest in the Middle East, don't present a very rosy picture at the moment," responded Alex.

Allison shared that she still was ten or more years from even considering retirement. Although tenured, she had been denied promotion to full professor six years ago owing to a publication record that the committee felt was underwhelming at the time. Unknown to the committee was that during this period she was ensnarled in a contentious divorce with her philandering husband. Her research had suffered from the distraction of the divorce and was reflected in her productivity. To add insult to injury, according to North Carolina law, her husband was entitled to one-half of her retirement savings and she to one-half of his. Unfortunately, as a physical therapist, he never was able to hold down any job long enough to be eligible for any significant retirement benefits and relied entirely on Allison for their medical coverage and living expenses. Allison now divorced and alone, came to the realization that she would have to teach many more years in order to replace the lost retirement revenue.

The new hire, Terry Swanson, appeared anxious at the tenor of the discussion and wondered what kind of a retirement he would have many years in the future. "I have never given much thought to what my retirement might be like. For me, it will be such a long time before that even becomes an issue. Thirty or forty years from now, who knows what the world will be like? Will universities as we now know them cease to exist, or will they morph into some hybrid form of cyberlearning? I'm just happy to have a job now and plan to take it one year at a time and hope for the best. I hope that when my time comes there is something left in social security and in my retirement plan to allow me to live a modest, but comfortable, life."

"Terry, how were you able to land your job at Ashmore?" asked Alex.

"Actually, I found it through Academic Appointment Placement Services, an employment agency located in Stone Mountain, Georgia. They gave me a heads up when this position opened and I applied immediately. When I read the ad for the position it was remarkable how closely my research and teaching interests mirrored what they were looking for. They narrowed it down to four other candidates, but fortunately for me, I got the offer and jumped on it immediately. I feel a little guilty about the job though, as I suspect I am the replacement for Professor Emerson, who died in that unfortunate boating accident."

"You shouldn't feel that way, Terry. It was a regrettable accident and you just happened to be at the right place at the right time," said Parker.

Alex didn't say anything, but couldn't help but wonder was this just a fortuitous circumstance or was there something sinister going on? He was more determined than ever to examine Paul Armstrong's Jaguar before he left Ashmore.

The conversation abruptly shifted to more mundane matters concerning Ashmore's new fund drive, the basketball program, and the large influx of foreign students and their assimilation into the student body, which was viewed positively by all those present at the commons table. After a final cup of coffee, Alex and Chris excused themselves and left the Union Building. It was still a bright, sunny day with the whole afternoon remaining.

As they walked back to their motel, Alex suggested that now would be a good time to go with him to inspect Paul Anderson's wrecked car at the Alpine Auto Salvage yard.

"Of course, Alex, but I'm not sure what you expect to find. Perhaps it was just a bona-fide accident after all. You're becoming paranoid about this accident."

"Just humor me Chris; it's only a short drive from our hotel. I just have to have a look and satisfy myself that there was no foul play."

Chris agreed, and soon they were heading out Highway 421 in the rented SUV.

CHAPTER 7: PARANOIA OR REALITY?

The sign along the side of Highway 421 directed them to a poorly-maintained gravel road that led to the Alpine Auto Salvage shop. As they pulled up to the concrete building with its peeling orange paint, Alex commented that it looked exactly the way it did years ago. This junk yard had been a gold mine for used auto parts for Alex's old Toyota pickup truck during his early days at Ashmore. As they entered the shop, Alex was surprised to see that Tommy Thompson, looking as surly as ever, was still at the front desk. Tommy recognized Alex and blurted out "What the hell are you doing here? You know all sales are final," and he laughed loudly.

"Good to see you again, you old reprobate. So, how's business?"

"Can't complain as long as people keep crashing their cars. This economy has a lot of people looking for used parts to keep their clunkers going for a few more miles. Who's that with ya?"

"Tommy, meet Chris Carpenter. He was a colleague of mine when I taught at Ashmore."

"Well, what can I do for you fellas?"

"We're here to take a look at a wrecked XKE Jaguar that was brought here a week or so ago. One of our good friends was killed in that crash."

"Sorry to hear that. That car was smashed up as bad as I have ever seen. Let me show you where it is."

They left the store and walked behind the shop to a fenced-in area where recent wrecks were being processed.

"You know it is kinda strange that you want to see that particular wreck. There was a fella in here last week asking for a used master cylinder for a XKE Jaguar. What are the odds of that? This is the only XKE Jaguar that I have ever had in my shop. That's really quite a coincidence, ain't it?"

"I'm not sure it was a coincidence, Tommy. That's why I'm here. I knew the owner of this car, and I'm convinced that he wouldn't have ignored any repairs that might have caused him to wreck."

As they approached the car, Alex was struck by how horrible the crash must have been to twist and distort the car so much that it was almost unrecognizable as a Jaguar. The hood was propped up against the wreck with the motor exposed. Alex could see where the master cylinder had been removed, but with the hydraulic brake line left intact. Alex bent the line down until a small amount of fluid dripped from the open end. Alex rubbed the fluid between his fingers. He knew it was not only brake fluid in the line but what he believed was motor oil.

"Tommy, what does this feel like to you?"

"It sure as hell doesn't feel like brake fluid."

Chris, who had remained a silent bystander until now, spoke up, "So how could that have anything to do with the accident?"

"You never allow motor oil to ever get into the master cylinder. If you do, it is only a matter of time before the rubber seals in the brake components swell or deform, and that can make your brakes stick, leak, or even fail. Paul would never let that happen.

This was no accident. Tommy, did the guy who bought the master cylinder pay by credit card or check?"

"No, it was strictly a cash sale. I had never seen the guy in these parts before."

"I'm sure we would never be able to convince the police that this wasn't an accident, and with no way to identify the guy who bought the master cylinder, I guess we are at a dead end. It's a damn shame, for I'd love to get my hands on the son of a bitch that did this. But what possible motive could be behind this senseless murder? I can't imagine anyone with a reason to kill Paul."

"Maybe you weren't being paranoid after all," said Chris.

Alex took his cell phone and snapped a few shots of the wreck before they walked back to the car.

"Chris, I don't see any point in telling Paul's wife about my suspicions. Alice has been through enough already. However, with the recent faculty deaths of Michael Emerson and Susan Sullivan, I'm convinced that something fishy is going on, and I'm determined to find out what it is. These aren't random deaths."

They walked back to their SUV, bid farewell to Tommy, and headed back to their hotel. Tomorrow would be a full day of alumni activities. Perhaps Alex could find some relief from his mounting concerns, if only for a few days.

CHAPTER 8: THE REUNION

It was glorious fall weather for the class reunion. The day was filled with activities beginning with a buffet breakfast in Addison Alumni Hall hosted by Ashmore's President, Dr. Warren H. Taft. President Taft presented his State of the University address highlighting the new University initiatives, including the expanded studies abroad program, the new Biological Sciences Building, and the ambitious new capital campaign targeting 500 million dollars in contributions.

Two athletic events coincided with the weekend reunion: a morning soccer match between the Ashmore Bobcats and the UNC Wilmington Seahawks, and an afternoon lacrosse match with the Mountaineers of nearby Appalachian State. Many departments, including the geology department, held small receptions for their graduates at noon that included a state-of-the-department speech by the chairman followed by a few selected student PowerPoint presentations, clearly a veiled attempt to entice financial support from the attending alumni. Following the departmental reception, Chris and Alex attended the lacrosse match with Appalachian State. Afterwards, now exhausted from a full day of activities, they returned to the hotel to rest before showering and dressing for the evening alumni reception.

A large tent had been set up in the main quad to host all the attending alumni for an early evening reception and sit-down dinner. Alex milled about the crowd at the reception and found many old acquaintances whom he had not seen in years. Alex thought how remarkable it was that many of his classmates had aged so gracefully while others could not be recognized until you read their name tags, and even then in disbelief. He sat at a table with one of his old basketball teammates, who was hardly recognizable with his shaved head and heavy beard and sporting an extra hundred pounds or more. But his laugh was, as always, hearty and contagious, accompanying stories long forgotten that brought back many memories and laughter that brought one to tears.

As the dinner drew to a close, the crowd was encouraged to stay and continue to mingle with old friends. The small four-piece band that had been playing "elevator music" during most of the dinner shifted to more lively hits from the sixties that drew dancing couples to the temporary wooden floor beneath the tent. Propane-powered heaters blew warm air into the tent to ameliorate the rapidly cooling evening air.

Alex continued to work the crowd looking for old acquaintances that he might have missed during the reception. He found several and enjoyed reminiscing about the "good old days" at Ashmore. Alex was startled by a hand firmly grasping his shoulder and turned to see Nolan Martin, one of his old fraternity brothers, who greeted him with a broad smile and the secret handshake of his fraternity. Nolan had aged well and appeared to be in excellent shape. His skin was tanned a golden brown, and he was decked out in the latest fashionable Miami Beach attire. Alex thought, *he must work out!*

"Damn, it's good to see you, Alex. It's been years since we have spoken. I heard that you had retired and were living in Hilton Head. How are Victoria and the kids?"

"She's fine, and the kids are now out on their own. How about you?"

"Still divorced, but enjoying my life as a bachelor in sunny Coral Gables, Florida. As you probably know, I completed my PhD in computer science at MIT. After working for IBM for ten years, I became disenchanted working for a big corporation. I founded my own company, Martin Security Services, which specialized in monitoring data storage systems of large corporations for malware or other nefarious hacking activities. A few years ago I was approached by a much larger company with an incredible offer to buy me out. As they say, they made me an offer I couldn't refuse. I decided to take the money and run to South Florida to enjoy my retirement in the Sunshine State. I spend most of my time now sailing in Biscayne Bay and scuba diving on Carysfort Reef."

Well, that explains the tan, thought Alex. Nolan excused himself when he spotted an old girlfriend across the room. Alex continued to mingle among the crowd until he saw another familiar face, Fred Jenkins, who had gone on to earn his doctorate in biological sciences at Stanford and currently holds a teaching position at a state university in Illinois.

"Aren't you ever going to retire, Fred?" asked Alex.

"Havin' too much fun. Besides can't afford to in this economy.   I'm at the mercy of our state teachers' pension fund, and I'm not sure that I can count on an adequate and stable retirement income."

"Let me ask you something, Fred. Have there been any unusual or suspicious deaths of your more senior active faculty in recent years?"

"I suppose you could call Carl Cummings' death last year a bit unusual."

"How's that?"

"Carl, who was an English professor, was on a Caribbean cruise last fall with his wife, celebrating their fiftieth wedding anniversary. According to his wife, Carl liked to take a late stroll around the ship before he turned in for the night. The sea was somewhat rough, and very few people were outside their rooms at that time of night. When he didn't return, Stella went looking for him and alerted the ship's staff. He was never found, and it was assumed that he had accidentally fallen overboard. No one reported seeing anything. His body was never recovered. The ship likely had travelled many miles before Stella alerted anyone. Such accidents are rare, but they do happen."

Alex couldn't help but wonder whether or not this was truly an accident.

Suddenly, she appeared out of the crowd. It was Pamela Morrison, Alex's first wife. The years had been kind to Pamela. She was still the knockout that had attracted Alex to her when they were undergrads at Ashmore. Pamela approached Alex with a broad smile on her face and gave him a peck on the cheek.

"Alex, it's so good to see you again after all these years. How have you been? How's your family? I assume you have one. Any children?"

"I'm fine Pam. I retired from Ashmore ten years ago and live in South Carolina on the coast. My wife, Victoria, and I have two girls, Allison and

Alisha. Both girls are married now and doing well. We also have two grandchildren. How about you?"

"Divorced and living alone. I don't know if you knew, but I married one of your old fraternity brothers, Jerry Summerland, who turned out to be a complete asshole. His real estate company folded during the last recession, and he began to drink excessively. When he drank, he became abusive. I had to take out a restraining order to keep him away. Our divorce was final six months ago, and I have been as free as a bird since then," she said as she snuggled up to Alex while sipping her drink

Alex suspected that she had already had too many drinks for her own good. Pam was clearly hitting on him, and he was becoming uncomfortable at the overt manner in which she was behaving.

"I'm really sorry that things didn't work out for you and Jerry, but I always thought he was a bit of jerk."

Ignoring the comment, Pamela whispered, "Alex, do you remember the good times we had when we were dating back here at Ashmore?" she said as she lost her balance and grabbed Alex's shoulder.

"I'm staying at the University Inn, Room 403, in case you're interested."

"Pam, you've had too much to drink. I'm sure it's the alcohol talking. I'm very flattered at the invitation. You're still a beautiful woman. I know it may sound corny, but I love my wife and respect her too much."

"Son of a bitch," slurred Pam. "You don't know what you're missing. I'd make it a night to remember."

"I'm sure you would, but I know that I would regret it in the morning."

Chris had been watching the two of them from afar and decided it was time to rescue his friend.

"Pamela, this is Chris, an old friend of mine from my teaching days here at Ashmore."

"Pleased to meet you, Chris. Your old buddy here and I go way back."

It was clear that Pamela was three sheets to the wind and could hardly stand on her own.

"Pamela, I think you've had enough for the night. Chris and I are also staying at the University

Inn and we can see that you get back to the hotel safely. We were about to leave anyway."

"Never mind me, I'm fine. I'll find my way back to the hotel. I just need another drink."

"Pamela, I insist. You really have had enough."

Reluctantly, Pamela agreed and the three left the reception. Alex hailed one of the taxis that had gathered at the campus bus stop near the reception tent to await fares. Within a few minutes they were back at the University Inn.

Alex left Chris in the lobby while he escorted Pamela to her room.

They rode the elevator up to the fourth floor, with Pamela holding on to Alex for support. She giggled a few times and kissed him on the neck. Alex didn't respond and soon they were at the door to her room. She fumbled through her purse until she found the electronic key card and swiped it several times before the door opened.

Pamela threw herself on the bed with her arms outstretched in a last ditch effort to seduce Alex.

"Last chance, Alex. You don't know what you're missing. It would be a night to remember."

Alex was tempted. She was still beautiful and as sexy as ever. After all, he rationalized, they had once been married. Alex felt himself aroused by her unabashed sexuality. He had never cheated on his wife before, but he was sorely tempted by this opportunity. On the brink of promiscuity, Alex's temptation was suppressed by the fact that he realized that he loved Victoria too much to betray her trust. Alex resisted the temptation.

"I'm more concerned about how I would feel in the morning. Good night, Pam. It was good to see you again," said Alex as he closed the door and returned to the elevator.

Chris was waiting in the lobby.

"I was beginning to worry. It was pretty obvious what she was up to. You're a good man, Alex."

"It's really sad seeing Pamela like that," said Alex, shaking his head. "Who knows what her life and mine would be like today if we had stayed married?"

"Forget about it, Alex. You couldn't possibly have done any better than Victoria. She's way above your pay grade," said Chris, as they both shared a nervous laugh.

There was a pot of complimentary coffee in the breakfast area of the lobby, available 24/7. Grabbing a cup of coffee, they found a quiet corner in the lobby and settled into two overstuffed leather chairs.

"I've been thinking a lot about Paul's so-called accident and the deaths of those other active members of the Ashmore faculty over the past year. I'm not sure that any of them were truly accidents, and I'm wondering if there is something more sinister going on. I find it strange that the replacement for Michael Emerson learned of the opening from the same company that found the slot for one of Ashmore's recent geology PhDs. It could just be a coincidence, but I want to do some more digging into the deaths of active faculty at other universities over the past year and see if anything suspicious turns up. As you say, I may be paranoid, but something just doesn't feel right to me."

"Alex, just to allay your concerns, it is only 150 miles from Augusta to Stone Mountain, Georgia, where Terry Swanson said that this AAPS company was located. Why don't I drive up there and check them out. I'll tell them I'm a retired faculty member and often get requests from former students for recommendations for teaching positions or inquiries as to whether or not I know of any openings from my personal contacts. I'll tell them that I heard about their company from Terry while we were having lunch at Ashmore. I'll suggest that perhaps I can point some of my former students in their direction. I'm sure they're always looking for new business. Maybe everything is on the up and up."

"I would really appreciate that, Chris. Thanks for humoring me. I'll keep you posted on what I have learned and check in with you after your trip to Atlanta."

After a brief conversation about mutual friends that they had seen at the reception, both men agreed it had been a full day and that it was time to turn in.

"Chris, let's meet for an early breakfast so that we can both get on the road and beat the crowd. I've got to drive back to the airport and turn in my rental car before I catch my early afternoon flight."

"Great. See you in the morning."

CHAPTER 9: MORE SUSPICIOUS DEATHS

Alex decided to skip the weekend traffic on the parkway and travelled the interstate back to the airport with time to spare after turning in his rental car and passing through security. Alex boarded the first leg of his flight to the Charlotte airport to connect with a small regional carrier bound for Savannah, where Victoria would be waiting to drive him home. The flight to Savannah was always a bumpy ride that made Alex nervous, although there never had been any plane crashes on that route that he was aware of. Once on the ground, a feeling of relief spread throughout his body as he hurried to the baggage claim area where Victoria was waiting.

"Honey, I'm so glad to see you," said Victoria. "How was the reunion?"

"It was great. Good to see Chris again as well as a lot of old friends that I had not seen since the last reunion ten years ago. Got a chance to visit the geology department and meet some of the graduate students. Chris and I also had lunch at the faculty commons and learned that not only Paul but two other active faculty members had died in accidents within the last year. Chris and I examined Paul's Jaguar, and I can tell you that his wreck was no accident. I have some serious doubts about the two other deaths as well but I have no proof to say that they weren't accidental. Did you talk to Alice? You didn't say anything to her about my suspicions, did you?"

"Of course not. She was obviously distraught, but seemed willing to accept that Paul's death was an unavoidable accident. I hope you're wrong about it not being an accident. Who would want to kill Paul?"

"I'm not sure yet, but I do have some suspicions about who might be responsible. I don't want to accuse anybody of being complicit in Paul's death without proof. Chris and I are following up on my hunch, and I have more research to do to see if I can dig up any evidence that supports my contention of foul play. Enough of this cloak and dagger stuff. I'm just so glad to see you. Have you heard from the girls? Any grandchildren news?"

With his arm around Victoria's shoulder, they continued their familial chatter until they arrived at their car, loaded Alex's baggage in the trunk, and drove to their seaside home in Hilton Head, only thirty-five miles away.

Later that afternoon, Alex checked out the countless number of emails that had accumulated during his absence, deleting most of them in short order. Once that burdensome task was completed, he began to search the Internet for online obituaries of recently deceased faculty at randomly selected universities scattered throughout the country. Most of the deaths listed were of emeriti professors in their late '70s and '80s and occasionally '90s, most of whom likely died of natural causes. Alex began to tabulate information on those faculty members who were actively teaching at the time of their deaths and who were more than seventy years of age.

Over the next several days, Alex began to see what he thought was an anomalously large number of such deaths attributed to older, actively teaching faculty. He summarized his findings in a terse, shortened format:

Colorado botany professor, age seventy-four. Died from gunshot wounds while hunting elk near Durango. Shot in the back by an unknown hunter. Ruled an accidental shooting despite fact that he was wearing high visibility clothing and his body was found in an open clearing.

Florida chemistry professor, age seventy-five. Died from exposure to small quantity of neurotoxin in university lab. Latex gloves he was wearing later discovered to be permeable to dimethylmercury. Ruled an accidental death despite the fact that he was an expert in toxic metal exposure.

Missouri history professor, age seventy-three. Died of a hit–and-run bicycle accident on a rural secondary road. An experienced cyclist who lived fifteen miles from her campus office and rode her bike to work every day, weather permitting. Debris from automobile believed to be responsible found at scene. No link to the automobile or its driver ever found.

Oregon physics professor, age eighty-two. Died from fall in stairwell after elevator serving his fourth floor office was unexpectedly out of service. Elevator was found to have frayed electrical wires resulting in shut-down. Fall was ruled accidental as he had suffered from severe vertigo and likely lost his balance.

Nevada philosophy professor, age seventy-nine. Death related to Mojave rattlesnake bite. Body found at residence. Death considered unusual as Mojave rattlesnakes had never been found previously in this part of Nevada. Snake was discovered in flower bed that had been recently attended to, presumably by victim.

California political science professor, age seventy-four. Died from rock climbing fall in Yosemite attributed to failure of faulty webbing in quickdraw. Was an experienced climber and in good physical condition for his age.

North Dakota engineering professor, age seventy-nine. Died of fatal burns when transferring t-butyl lithium from one sealed container to another in chemistry laboratory. A defective syringe used in the transfer was blamed for the accidental spill that ignited his clothing. He was not wearing his protective lab coat at the time of the accident.

Minnesota psychology professor, age eighty. Died during a routine medical procedure in an out-patient clinic during administration of bacterially contaminated anesthesia.

Illinois civil engineering professor, age eighty-two. Death resulted from smoke inhalation in house fire. Investigators ruled fire caused by faulty electrical wiring. House had recently been renovated and new electrical circuitry had been installed.

Alex wondered if all of these deaths were merely fortuitous accidents, or if any of these deaths were contrived.

Alex decided to try another approach in his analysis of older active faculty deaths. He returned to the obituary websites of all those universities that he had already surveyed, and tabulated similar deaths of active faculty over the previous five years. He found a dramatic increase in the number of such deaths in the last two years. These results fueled his conviction that there had indeed been foul play, but proving it was an entirely different matter. Could there be a link between these deaths and the AAPS Company, or was Alex just being paranoid again?

Alex accessed the Academic Appointment Placement Services website that was extremely well designed and had numerous links to job opportunities. One link was to recently hired AAPS clients and the institutions that had hired them. Alex surveyed the list to see if any of the positions vacated by the older faculty who had died in the last two years had been filled by any of the AAPS clients. He chose ten deaths randomly from his compilation. Of these ten deaths, four of the potential faculty openings had not as yet been posted, two positions were advertised as active searches, and four were found on the AAPS list of successful placements. While not overwhelmingly convincing, finding four of the ten linked to AAPS seemed very suspicious, even more so when considering that four openings had not as yet been posted. Perhaps some of those would be ultimately linked to AAPS when they were filled.

It was one thing to have your suspicions aroused even more so than before, but what good would it do to continue searching for potentially suspicious deaths if nothing could be proven?

I only hope that Chris's visit to AAPS might give us something to go on, thought Alex as he shut down his laptop, walked to the window, fixated on the waves breaking against the seawall that sheltered his home, and pondered what his next step would be.

CHAPTER 10: AAPS HEADQUARTERS

After returning from the reunion, Chris spent the first week at home catching up on his honey-do projects for Marilyn and the second week searching the Internet for more information on the Academic Appointment Placement Services Corporation. He learned that AAPS was actually a small subsidiary of a much larger corporation, Noble Cloud Computing Inc., based at the same address in Stone Mountain, Georgia. According to their website, Noble provided secure data storage services for several Fortune 500 companies.

Chris wasn't all that familiar with what cloud computing actually was and spent considerable time on the Internet trying to understand it better. He learned that cloud computing in its simplest terms refers to storing and accessing data and programs, not on your hard drive, but rather on the Internet. Although he emerged from his research with only a vague understanding of the complexities of cloud computing, he felt that he knew enough to ask reasonably intelligent questions when he visited the Noble Cloud Computing Company.

Chris also learned that Noble had established itself as an important player in crowd computing by blending its cloud computing capabilities with crowdsourcing platforms, collaboration packages, and information sharing applications, such as SharePoint, blogs, social networks, Twitter, and Flickr to find solutions to complex problems utilizing the combined knowledge, intelligence, and life experiences of the crowd.

The following Monday morning, Chris said goodbye to Marilyn and began his drive north from Augusta to Atlanta on Interstate 20. Traffic was especially heavy that morning, and Chris was more nervous than usual as he competed with the commuters and the eighteen-wheelers that exceeded the sixty-five mph limit and jockeyed for position in the fastest-moving lanes. In addition, sporadic morning showers limited visibility. Now that Chris was in his late seventies, he no longer felt comfortable dueling with fellow road warriors and was already looking forward to returning to the quiet suburbs of Augusta. After what seemed like an eternity, Chris exited Interstate 20 and continued on Interstate 285 until arriving at the Stone Mountain exit ramp. It was only a few miles to Stone Mountain Industrial Park where he found a large, modern commercial building wrapped in tinted windows that overlooked meticulously manicured landscaping. A tasteful sign out front indicated that the building housed Noble Cloud Computing.

Chris realized that this was a much larger enterprise than he had envisioned, as he walked towards the massive plate-glass doors that opened automatically as he neared the entrance. The lobby was expansive, with wood-paneled walls that featured numerous watercolor and oil paintings by notable local artists. A large circular reception desk was manned by a uniformed, armed guard who rose from his chair and greeted Chris as he approached, "May I help you, sir?"

"Indeed you may. I was wondering if there is a representative of your academic placement services that I could speak to. I am a retired professor and only recently learned of the service you're providing for doctoral students who aspire to teach. One of my former students has been looking for a position for several years."

"I see, sir. And what is your name?"

"Dr. Christopher Carpenter. I am a retired professor from Ashmore University in North Carolina."

"Thank you. Please sign in with your signature as well as your printed name, the time of day, and the department you wish to visit in this visitor ledger. After signing in, take a seat in the lobby until I check with the appropriate personnel for approval of your visit."

Christopher took a seat in the lobby, out of earshot of the receptionist who picked up the desk phone and placed a call.

"Roger, this is Carl at the front desk. I have a guy here who says he is a retired professor and wants to talk to somebody in the AAPS division. His name is Christopher Carpenter. Says he taught at Ashmore University in North Carolina. Shall I give him a visitor's pass and send him on up?"

"No, Carl, let him sit there until I check him out."

Roger Anderson, who had been in charge of the AAPS division since its inception, entered Christopher Carpenter's name into their extensive database of information for present and past faculty members in all the colleges and universities in North America and Canada. He scrolled through two pages of data outlining Chris's educational background, the courses he had taught at Ashmore, at what age he had retired, and information concerning his membership in Alcoholics Anonymous while at Ashmore.

Roger wondered if there were other reasons for Dr. Carpenter's visit. Although he looked harmless enough on paper, Roger decided that he should meet with him to determine if there was more to his visit than meets the eye.

He picked up the phone, dialed the reception desk, and told Carl to issue him a visitor's pass.

Roger said he would be down shortly to meet Dr. Carpenter in the lobby and arrange for him to take the standard public tour of their facility.

Chris sat patiently in the lobby, perusing the pile of outdated magazines on the table beside him, until Roger finally appeared and greeted him with a firm handshake.

"Dr. Carpenter, it's a pleasure to meet you. I'm Roger Anderson, head of the AAPS Division. How can I be of assistance?"

"I recently attended a class reunion at Ashmore University in North Carolina and had a chance to visit my old department and spoke with some of the PhD students who told me about your company and how you have been assisting them in finding job opportunities. I was passing through Atlanta on my way to visit relatives in North Carolina and thought I might stop by and learn more about your services."

"Happy to oblige, Dr. Carpenter. Let's go up to my office where we will be more comfortable. But before we do, I would appreciate it if you would leave your cell phone here with Carl until your visit is over. We are extremely sensitive to the privacy requirements of our clientele and do not permit cell phone photos to be taken anywhere within our facility. I'm sure you understand."

"Of course," said Chris as he handed his iPhone to Carl for safekeeping.

Chris followed Roger to an elevator that could only be accessed by a security card swiped through a reader. They entered the elevator and exited on the tenth floor. As they walked down the hallway past a few offices with open doors, Chris was struck by the large number of monitors that lined the office walls, displaying Excel spreadsheets and maps with locations highlighted with multi-colored pinpoints. Chris made no comment as they made their way to Roger's well-appointed corner office, which had a commanding view of Stone Mountain in the distance.

"What a spectacular view of Stone Mountain!" gushed Christopher.

"Yes, it is. I'm quite busy, Dr. Carpenter, so let's get down to business. Tell me what you have heard about the services we provide based on your conversation with the students."

"Well, it is my understanding that you closely monitor openings in academic departments in all the disciplines around the country and, for a fee, attempt to match up your clients with the available positions. I understand that there is an up-front fee of $5,000 that is returned if your organization is unable to secure a position for that client within the first year. I also understand that if you are successful in securing a position for your client they are obligated to pay you one month's salary during their first year of employment."

"Well, Dr. Carpenter, you are well informed about our services. But I think you also realize, now that you have seen our corporate offices, that there's no way we could make much of a profit from such an enterprise. We generate our primary income from our Noble Computing clients who need extensive and confidential cloud data storage as well as other data-mining services that we provide. We operate AAPS at a significant loss."

"But then, may I ask, why are you doing it?"

"Our founder and CEO, Dr. Malcolm Fowler, has been concerned for some time about the quality of education in our country extending from elementary schools all the way through graduate schools. Globally we have lost our edge in basic sciences and math. Malcolm believes that the infusion of new blood at the college level, in the long run, will help rectify this problem.

"We provide a very valuable service by screening the available graduates from our doctoral programs and helping them link up with positions that will benefit both the client and the university the most. Dr. Fowler believes that although the experience of an aging faculty is a valuable asset, it pales by comparison with the enthusiasm, the vigor, and the contemporary perspective that today's PhDs can bring to the classroom. The educational landscape is rapidly changing as new cyberlearning courses are being included in the curriculum, but in Malcolm's opinion, a televised image remotely transmitted is no substitute for a vibrant, real-life professor in the classroom.

"It may interest you to know that in most cases we actually refund the initial $5,000 fee to the client and waive the requirement to pay us one month's academic salary during their first year. Our fee structure is designed to identify those most serious about pursuing a career in academia and to weed out those who would be better served in other professions.

"Our computational capacity is enormous. We have access to the personal records of all active faculty regarding their educational backgrounds, courses taught, publications, society memberships, research funding profiles, number of graduate students advised, personal data such as date of birth, marital status, awards and accomplishments, to name but a few of our capable sources of information. If a faculty member has a Facebook page, tweets, or twitters, we know about it. We have created a crowdsourcing website which lists all active faculty members in America where students can add comments about any professor's course that they took including the quality of the course and the benefit that the course accrued to them—effectively, this is a very extensive teacher-course evaluation. We also monitor retirements, obituaries in all relevant newspapers, and announcements of any new faculty openings. We work closely with virtually all the universities and professional associations because the work we do is in their best interest as well."

"Roger, I must say that I'm a bit overwhelmed and very impressed with what you've told me. When I first learned of your service, I frankly was concerned that the students might be, and I hesitate to use the word, scammed."

"I can see how you might misconstrue our intentions. But I hope your visit to our facility and my comments have allayed your fears about the true mission of AAPS. I apologize, Dr. Carpenter, but I have some other rather important business to take care of today, but I will have my administrative assistant take you on a tour of the non-confidential portions of our facility. Much of what we do here must be kept in the strictest of confidence and can never be disclosed to the public if we are to maintain our integrity. I'm sure you understand."

"Of course. I realize how busy you are and appreciate your taking the time to speak with me."

Roger pushed the intercom button on his desk and summoned Alice, his administrative assistant, to accompany Dr. Carpenter on a tour of the facility. The two shook hands and parted company upon the arrival of Alice. After Chris left, Roger picked up the phone and dialed Malcolm Fowler's private line.

"Malcolm, a retired professor from Ashmore University just left my office. I'm having Alice take him on the public tour of our facility. I'm not sure that he is any threat to us, but I have to admit that I'm a little puzzled by his visit. His comment that he thought the students were possibly being scammed by us disturbed me. I think we should keep an eye on him for a while to see if anything suspicious develops."

"I agree. Be sure and have Marty see to it that our electronic monitoring program is embedded in his cell phone before he retrieves it."

"I'll call security now and get the chip installed in his cell phone before he finishes the tour."

"Good. Keep me posted."

Roger dialed the company's security center and asked for Marty McIver, his most trusted employee. A Desert Storm veteran and previously convicted computer hacker, Marty was told to modify Chris's cell phone with encrypted listening and tracking capabilities as well as with remote control of his cell phone camera, a technology recently acquired from a Chinese subsidiary of Noble Computing.

"Marty, be sure that you make the necessary modifications before he returns to the information desk. He is presently touring the building with Alice."

"No problem, Roger."

"Thanks, Marty."

The tour with Alice lasted for approximately an hour. Chris was dazzled by the magnitude of the computational power that Noble Computing possessed, with row after row of state-of-the-art servers attesting to enormous storage and back-up capabilities. Alice assured Chris that all of their data storage was extremely secure and that there had been no unauthorized breaches to their clients' data files. At the end of the tour, Alice accompanied Chris to the main lobby information desk where he retrieved his cell phone. He returned to the parking lot, started up his car, and began his drive back to Augusta.

As it was still early in the afternoon, the traffic wasn't particularly heavy. Chris stopped for gasoline at one of the large truck stops along the interstate and grabbed a pre-packaged sandwich and a Coke. He sat alone at one of the outside tables off to one side, and decided to give Alex a call to tell him what he had learned at AAPS. He dialed Alex, unaware that his cell phone would transmit his GPS location, all calls, text messages, emails, and Internet searches to a monitoring server at Noble Computing, where they would be stored to be accessed by the company at will. By chance, Roger was checking Chris's cellphone to see if the tracking program was functioning properly just as Chris dialed Alex. Roger immediately knew that Chris wasn't headed north to visit relatives in North Carolina as he had said, but instead, was headed south toward Augusta.

Roger listened intently as he monitored the call.

"Hello, Alex. Chris here. I'm on my way back home. I had a good visit at AAPS and…."

Alex interrupted, "Chris, you're breaking up. I can't understand a word you're saying. Call me when you get back home."

Chris couldn't make out what Alex was saying, but assumed from Alex's garbled message that there was a transmission problem and turned off his cellphone.

After the signal was lost, Roger wondered whom Chris was calling so soon after his visit to Noble Computing, and what the reason for the call was. He decided that further monitoring of Chris's phone was in order until he was satisfied that there was no further need for concern.

It was late afternoon by the time Chris pulled into his driveway in Augusta. He was exhausted from the round-trip drive to and from Stone Mountain in a single day. Marilyn greeted Chris at the door and asked him how his trip went.

"It was productive, but I'm really bushed. I just can't take these long trips by car anymore. My meeting at AAPS was very interesting, and so far as I was able to determine, they seem to be on the up and up. They're really just a small subsidiary of a much larger computing company that seems to be providing a valuable service by helping doctoral students find academic positions. I think Alex is way off base thinking that this company is responsible for any of the deaths of senior faculty who just happened to be actively teaching in their seventies and eighties. I think the link that Alex sees between what he refers to as "suspicious deaths" of senior faculty and their positions subsequently being filled by clients of AAPS is purely fortuitous. I don't think there's any kind of a conspiracy going on, and I'm going to tell him so. I couldn't reach him on my cell phone earlier today. I'll just give him a call later tonight after supper. Do I have time for a short nap before supper, honey?"

"Of course you do. You just relax, and I'll call you when supper's ready."

After supper, using his landline rather than his cell, Chris called Alex and told him basically what he had told Marilyn. He said that he had discovered nothing suspicious during his visit to AAPS, and attempted to convince Alex that he was being paranoid.

"I can appreciate how you feel, Chris, but I've been doing more research since we last spoke, and I'm convinced that there is something going on that's not right. I don't believe that the Ashmore deaths are a coincidence. I have uncovered several suspicious cases at other universities, and I intend to pursue them further. I appreciate that you took the time to visit their headquarters. Apparently they are very good at convincing people that they are merely providing a beneficial service for young, aspiring doctoral students. I admit that I may be barking up the wrong tree, but I have to see this through. I know you don't agree with me, old friend, but I'll stay in touch. If I am wrong, I'll be the first to admit it. Just humor me a little longer."

"Just don't say that I didn't warn you, Alex. I hate to see you wasting time on such a futile endeavor. Look at it this way. Old folks die every day, including old faculty members. When they do, their deaths create employment opportunities for enthusiastic new grads who bring youthful energy to the classroom. So, all in all, it's not a bad trade-off. It's just a fact of life, and I don't think there's anything sinister going on."

"I can understand your position, Chris. So let's just leave it at that. I've got my teeth into this thing, and I'm not ready to let go. If I'm right, we're talking about a criminal enterprise that involves murdering innocent people. If I'm wrong, there's no harm done, and I'll be happy to admit that I was mistaken. But I don't think I'm wrong. You know I am very sympathetic to the plight of graduating doctoral students who have sacrificed an enormous amount just to have an opportunity to teach, but I don't want that opportunity to derive from the suffering and premature death of others. I'll keep you posted. Please give my best to Marilyn. Goodbye," said Alex abruptly ending the conversation.

Chris hung up the phone and said, "Damn, Marilyn. Alex is one pigheaded guy. I have never seen that side of him before. He is a 'Damn the torpedoes! Full speed ahead!' kind of guy. I just hope that he isn't wasting his time 'chasing windmills'."

"Oh, dear. Just be patient with Alex. He has always been a good friend of yours. I'm sure he'll come to his senses in time. How about a cup of tea?"

"Don't mind if I do. Anything good on the TV tonight?"

"Probably not, dear. But it really doesn't matter. You always fall asleep by nine o'clock anyway," said Marylyn as Chris smiled and settled into his overstuffed leather chair.

CHAPTER 11: CONTINUING SEARCH FOR THE TRUTH

Over the next month, Alex was relentless in his search for other suspicious deaths of senior faculty who were still actively teaching. Even his wife, Victoria, was concerned about his obsession that these deaths were not accidental but was unable to deter him from spending so many hours every day on the Internet. Alex was frustrated when he found no reasonable way to determine whether these deaths were actually murders, or whether they resulted from purely natural causes. He needed to find a way to link the deaths to AAPS if indeed there was any such connection. Alex spent many hours trying to come up with a way to make this connection and finally concluded that the only way he could do so was to somehow hack into their computer system. He was fully cognizant that this would be an extremely challenging task, considering the extensive firewalls that Noble Computing likely had installed to protect their databases. Alex reasoned that inasmuch as AAPS was using its cloud crowdsourcing website to evaluate faculty, it likely was the most vulnerable component in Noble's computing system.

Alex recalled his conversation at the Ashmore reunion reception with Nolan Martin, one of his fraternity buddies and the founder of a highly successful computer security company. He wondered if Nolan would be willing to advise him as to whether or not hacking into AAPS's open source data base without detection would be possible, and if he were caught, what the potential criminal consequences might be. Aside from that, Alex also wondered what the chances were that he himself might become a victim of a "fatal accident" if his hacking attempt was detected by AAPS.

Alex initially thought he would look up Nolan's phone number on the Internet, but worried that his computer might eventually be hacked by AAPS and lead directly to Nolan. He couldn't help but wonder if indeed he wasn't becoming overly paranoid, as Chris had suggested. Alex remembered that at the reunion reception Nolan had given him a business card which contained his email address as well as his home and mobile phone numbers. After a few frustrating minutes searching through the clutter on his desk, he uncovered Nolan's business card. Paranoia began to settle in again as Alex wondered whether he should use his home phone or his mobile phone. He had read about the Internet of Everything (IoE) where electronic devices, networks, and clouds would ultimately all be connected and present significant security challenges. He realized that he was becoming irrational and that such vulnerability was something to worry about in the future, but not now. He decided to use his landline because he knew it was more secure than a cellphone.

He dialed Nolan at his home phone number in Miami and got no answer. He then tried his cell and reached him as he was having lunch at a local seaside restaurant on Key Biscayne with a friend.

"Nolan. This is Alex Chandler. Do you have a few minutes? I really need to get your advice."

"Alex, what a surprise hearing from you. I'm just finishing my lunch with a friend. Let me call you back in a few minutes."

"I'm sorry to disturb you, Nolan. Perhaps I should call you later."

"No problem, Alex. I'll ring you back after I finish my lunch."

"I'm at home. Call me on my landline. Let me give you my number."

Nolan jotted down Alex's number, and assured him that he would call him back shortly. Alex had second thoughts as he waited for Nolan to return his call. He didn't want to get Nolan involved in something that could potentially be dangerous if his suspicions were correct. On the other hand, perhaps Nolan could confirm Chris's belief that there was nothing sinister going on at AAPS, and put Alex's fears to rest. It seemed like an eternity, but after a few minutes Nolan returned his call.

"Well, Alex, what's up?"

"I hate to bother you, Nolan, but I think I have stumbled onto something that may involve murders that are being covered up as accidental deaths. My good friend Chris, whom you met at the reunion, thinks I'm being paranoid and that I'm just letting my imagination run wild. That may be the case, but the more I dig into this, the more it appears clear to me that there's something going on. It involves older faculty members who are still actively teaching but who are dying under very mysterious circumstances."

Alex then outlined for Nolan the whole set of circumstances that led him to his conclusion that these deaths were not accidental. At first, Nolan was incredulous, but the more Alex disclosed about his findings, the more he became convinced that Alex might be onto something. When Nolan learned that the company under suspicion was a subsidiary of Noble Cloud Computing, he interrupted Alex.

"Damn, what a coincidence. I'm very familiar with Noble Cloud Computing. They're the company that I sold my business to... including all my proprietary software and security systems. If you're up against Noble, you are up against some pretty heavy hitters in the computer security business."

"Well, Nolan, that brings me to the reason for my call. I feel a little uncomfortable asking you this, but do you think there's any possible way that one could hack into the AAPS computer database without being detected?"

"If you're asking me whether or not it is possible for you to tap into that database, the answer is unequivocally no way in hell. Noble has one of the most sophisticated security systems in the entire industry and has developed proprietary firewalls that even I couldn't breach. On the other hand, you mentioned that AAPS had a crowdsourcing website where outsiders could enter opinions on faculty from whom they had taken courses. Since this is a website that would not require heavy-duty security, perhaps it is vulnerable if they are using lower-level firewalls. I'm not saying that it can be done, but I may take a crack at it to see if it's possible."

"Nolan, I'm concerned that I might be exposing you to danger if my suspicions are correct. If you start nosing around in their business and they find out, I'm sure they wouldn't hesitate to eliminate you. I don't want that on my conscience. I can't ask you to take that risk."

"Alex, don't forget I know how to conceal my hacking queries by routing my searches through several international IP addresses. I suspect that the secondary firewalls they are using to protect the crowdsourcing blog are those that I developed before

I sold my company to them. I know how security systems work well enough to know when I'm close to being detected and can vanish electronically in an instant. Let me give it a crack."

Reluctantly, Alex relented but asked Nolan not to take any unnecessary chances on his behalf.

"To play it safe, I'll send you via snail mail a list of twenty or so suspicious deaths that should be stored in Noble's database. See if you can find anything strange about their entries."

"No sweat, Alex. I'll get back in touch with you after I've had a chance to examine the vulnerability of AAPS's crowdsourcing website and see if I can find those professors on your list," said Nolan as he hung up the phone.

Meanwhile back at Noble Computing's headquarters, Marty McIver was continuing to monitor records of the tracking software that he had installed in Chris's cellphone. Marty could find nothing of value in his cellphone records. There were only text messages and phone calls to family members and a few local businesses. Nothing out of the ordinary. There was nothing to suspect that Chris had any ulterior motives for his recent visit to Noble Headquarters. He was about to notify Malcolm that he felt there was no further reason to monitor Chris's activity, when he noticed that an unanswered call had come through recently from a number in Hilton Head, South Carolina. No message had been left. Marty searched for the number in Noble Computing's massive database and quickly discovered that the number was for a cellphone registered to an Alex Chandler.

Now that Marty had Alex's cellphone number, it was a fairly simple matter to see if the subscriber identity module (SIM) card in his phone was vulnerable to hacking by sending two text messages (SMS) to see if it lacked a secure data encryption standard (DES). Fortunately for Alex, his relatively new cellphone was protected by an up-to-date encryption system, much to the dismay of Marty.

Marty thought it was time to find out whom they were dealing with and entered Alex's name in the company's proprietary search engine. He quickly learned of Alex's industrial background, his teaching career at Ashmore, his family, numerous details about his financial situation, and his medical history. He discovered that Alex had undergone surgery for a heart valve replacement three years ago, an issue that might come in handy if they were to find out that he had been prying into Noble's business.

CHAPTER 12: A CHINK IN THE SECURITY ARMOR

It was several days before Alex's listing of suspicious deaths arrived at Nolan's Miami home. Nolan perused the list and found it included faculty from a variety of disciplines and covered a wide geographic range as well. Nolan began his search of Noble Computing's database by assuming a fictitious name. After routing his entry through multiple servers including several located overseas, he accessed the AAPS website for evaluating the quality of a professor's teaching ability. He selected a biology professor's course in invertebrate zoology at Michigan State University. Nolan fabricated answers to the questionnaire that was required before one could enter comments. Once the website dedicated to that specific course and professor had been accessed, Nolan used different hacking approaches in his attempts to enter the entire listing for all of the professors that comprised the database. After a few preliminary attempts had been thwarted, Nolan was denied access by a more sophisticated firewall that he recognized as one that he had personally developed and that had been acquired by Noble Computing upon the sale of his company.

Nolan struggled to remember how he was able to breach the firewall during the testing phase. After several attempts he was frustrated by how rusty he had become. Suddenly he broke through the firewall, and a large data file began to scroll down his screen. Nolan quickly linked the data file to his high capacity external drive and began to copy the files. He could see that he was nearing the end of the alphabetically listed file when suddenly his screen began to flicker and went blank. It was clear that he had been detected, and Noble was trying to determine the location of his IP address.

Better get the hell out of here pretty damn quick! thought Nolan as he began to cover his tracks by routing his shutdown through servers in China, Russia, England and Germany. *That should do it. There's no way in hell they're going to find me,* as he turned off his computer and disconnected the external drive.

Nolan maintained another high-end computer as a stand-alone that was intentionally designed to be inaccessible via the Internet. He plugged in the external drive containing the AAPS database and, with Alex's list in hand, began to search the listing for those individuals that Alex had earmarked for scrutiny. It wasn't long before he noticed that virtually all of them had the peculiar file extension ".htl", an extension not present on most of the other entries. Some of the names with the ".**htl**" notation were also displayed in bold text. He wondered what the ".htl" extension stood for and why some were highlighted and others not.

Back at Noble Computing, Marty and his surveillance crew persisted for more than an hour in their attempts to establish who had cracked their security system, but had no success. Frustrated with the failure of their security firewall to prevent this intrusion into their presumably secure database, as well as with their inability to determine the culprit responsible for this breach, Marty, visibly shaken, his face reddened with rage, blurted out in anger:

"Whoever accessed our database knows what the hell he is doing and is pretty adept at covering his tracks. Damn it! Review the security system controlling the faculty database to see if we can strengthen the site with a more sophisticated firewall. Someone is hell-bent on mining these data. I don't know if it is just curiosity, a prank, or someone with an ulterior motive. Stay on high alert in case any other attempts occur. Malcolm isn't going to be too happy about this."

Nolan decided not to contact Alex for several days after his successful hacking of the AAPS database. He had to be reasonably confident that Noble had not been successful in tracing the hacking back to his computer. Besides, he wanted some time to try to determine the significance of the ".htl" designations before discussing his findings with Alex. He scrolled through the database and randomly selected several faculty names that had the ".htl" extension attached to their files. After determining where these individuals taught, what their ages were, and what was the sense of posted reviews as to their competency as teachers, Nolan searched the faculty databases at their institutions and found that all those listed in bold text were deceased, whereas all those not shown in bold text were still actively teaching. Nolan compiled a listing of several of the deceased faculty and accessed obituaries from their local newspapers. Many did not mention the cause of death. A few, however, did note circumstances of death that were interpreted as being accidental, such as automobile accidents, drownings, house fires, and heart attacks. If these deaths in fact had been orchestrated, nothing in these records provided any clue as to the real cause of death.

Nolan then filtered the data to show only those professors actively teaching who were at least seventy years old. The resultant list contained approximately a thousand entries. Most of those on the list did not have the ".htl" extensions, but a few hundred did. He compiled a list of those with ".htl" extensions and arranged them according to academic affiliation and found one such name on the list from Ashmore, a Professor Parker Johnson in the physics department. The ".**htl**" extension was in bold type.

Nolan began feeling confident that he had not been detected by Noble and decided to contact Alex to bring him up-to-date on what he had found. He dialed Alex on his landline as they had agreed for security reasons.

The ringing telephone roused Alex from a nap he was taking after falling asleep reading his favorite mystery writer's newest book. Alex stifled a yawn, gathered his senses, and finally answered the telephone.

"Alex here. Who's calling?"

"Alex, this is Nolan. I wanted to bring you up-to-date on what I've learned from the database that I was able to pirate from Noble Computing."

"Damn, Nolan, that's incredible! I can't believe you pulled that off. Are you sure you weren't detected?"

"Oh, I was detected all right, but I got the hell out of their site in short order, and I'm sure they weren't able to track the source of the hacking. The good news is that I was able to download all the data that they had in their faculty files and can tell you they had an enormous amount of information in that database. I found a very peculiar '.htl' extension on the files of several of the faculty that I have been unable to crack. Many of the actively teaching faculty who were at least seventy years old had that peculiar extension. Those designated with the extension highlighted in bold were all deceased with the time of death indicated. I found one such highlighted faculty member from our old alma mater Ashmore, a Professor Parker Johnson in the physics department. I assume that he has died, but I didn't find a date attached."

"Did you say Parker Johnson? Chris and I just had lunch with him the day before the reunion activities. He looked fine to me. I recall that he said he had no intention of retiring even though he was well into his seventies. Do you have any idea how he died?"

"Alex, there is no indication in the database as to the manner in which any of the faculty died. I think we ought to check with Ashmore to see what caused his death."

"I'll take care of it, Nolan. I wish I had been wrong about my suspicions, but what you have told me about the database leads me to believe that they were correct. Something's going on, and somehow Noble Computing is involved. Their role in this and their motive behind it are unclear. I'll get back to you as soon as I check out what happened to Parker. In the meantime, please copy the relevant files with the suspicious deaths on a flash drive and mail it to me."

CHAPTER 13: SUSPICIONS CONFIRMED

Over the next few days, Alex began to search the local obituaries in Waltonville's local paper, the *Mountaineer*. After searching the records as far back as the reunion date, he found no indication that Parker had died. Perhaps his death went unreported. Perhaps he was buried in another town. His curiosity got the best of him and he decided to try to call Parker's home in Waltonville. After finding the number on the Internet, Alex dialed the number and anxiously waited for someone to answer the phone.

"Hello, this is the Johnson residence. We're not able to take your call at this time, but if you leave...." The call was abruptly interrupted, "Hello, Parker Johnson here. Please wait until that damn recording finishes."

Thank God, he's alive, thought Alex as he waited for the recording to clear. Alex was caught off guard because he hadn't anticipated what he would say to Parker, who he had assumed was already dead.

"Parker, this is Alex Chandler. Perhaps you remember me. We had lunch together at the reunion last fall. How are you doing?" Alex was still at a loss for words.

"I'm fine Alex, what can I do for you?"

"I was concerned because I heard that you had had an accident of some sort and were in bad shape."

"No, no, I'm fine. I don't know how these rumors get started. As a matter of fact I'm about to embark on a trip to Sandia National Lab in Albuquerque, New Mexico. One of my former students is a post-doc there and is working on some new method for treating hazardous nuclear waste. He seems to think some of my early research on the subject might provide some insight into his new project. I worked at the lab part-time when I was a graduate student in the physics department at UNM and I'm really looking forward to seeing how much the facility has changed since I was there."

"Sounds like a great trip down memory lane. I'm sure you'll have a wonderful time reconnecting with your student, and I'm very sorry for bothering you with these false rumors of your failing health."

"Thanks for your concern anyway, Alex, but I'm fit as a fiddle as they say. Had a check-up with my doctor just last week and everything was fine. It was good to see you at the reunion. Now, I have to finish packing, as I leave tomorrow morning. I'm sure you understand."

"Of course, Parker. Have a good trip."

Alex hung up the phone, and wondered if he had misinterpreted the information gathered from the database that Nolan had accessed. Perhaps the ".**htl**" extensions in bold type did not indicate that those faculty entries were deceased. Could it be that there was nothing sinister contained in the Noble database, and he might be simply on a "wild-goose chase?" He decided to let his investigation rest for a while.

Over the next few weeks, Alex was content to work on one of his consulting projects and gave little thought to his suspicions of criminal activity by Noble Computing. His complacency was shattered when he received the latest alumni newsletter from Ashmore. It wasn't the highlights of activities by several members of the faculty that attracted his attention, but rather the memorial tribute to Parker Johnson, who had died from an apparent heart attack in Albuquerque, New Mexico. The attack occurred while Parker was riding the Sandia Peak Tramway that runs from the foothills east of Albuquerque to the crest of the Sandia Mountains. The Tramway is reported to be the longest in the world, spanning a distance of ten thousand feet. The attack apparently occurred while the tram was only halfway up the mountain. Paramedics had been alerted and were waiting when the tram reached the crest, but their attempts to revive him were futile. According to fellow passengers, the heart attack was sudden and with little warning. He fell to the floor after grabbing his chest.

Alex recoiled in anger; his thoughts now filled with rage. He was convinced that Parker's death was not an accident because he had been targeted in Noble's database well before the heart attack occurred. There was no telling how long his murder had been planned. Alex believed that the bastards at Noble were just looking for the right opportunity to eliminate Parker and they found it on the tramway. Alex speculated that someone must have injected him with a drug that induced the heart attack or drugged his food or drink somewhere along the way. It was now clear to Alex that there could be others in the

Noble database that have been targeted for killing but are still alive at the moment. It was only a matter of time before Noble's assassins would find the right opportunity to carry out their deadly missions. Alex's continued inability to find any bona fide evidence to prove his suspicions infuriated him. He knew everything that he had learned was purely circumstantial, and was beginning to feel more and more helpless against such a powerful adversary. Alex was so engrossed in his irrational obsession that he never really gave much thought to the fact that he was putting himself in great danger.

Alex decided that he would check in with Chris to alert him of his new findings. He now felt confident that his suspicions were valid based on Nolan's discovery that older faculty were being targeted for elimination by AAPS, and this was confirmed by the death of Parker Johnson. Alex dialed Chris on his home phone and learned from Marylyn that he was out running errands. He then decided to call him on his cell phone, not knowing that Chris's cell phone conversations were being monitored by Noble and recorded automatically.

"Chris, this is Alex. I want to bring you up-to-date on what I've learned about AAPS and their activities. I believe I now have conclusive proof that the faculty deaths that I've been investigating are in fact being orchestrated by Noble Computing."

"My God, Alex, I thought you had given up on your outlandish idea that these deaths were anything but accidental."

"No, my friend. I am more convinced now than ever that older tenured faculty are being targeted and systematically being murdered in creative ways that appear purely accidental. And there is no doubt in my mind that AAPS is entirely responsible. I have my old fraternity brother, Nolan Martin, to thank for that."

This inadvertent disclosure was one that Alex would live to regret.

Alex outlined in detail what he had learned from his research of faculty obituaries in universities throughout the country and confided in Chris what Nolan had discovered by hacking into Noble's computer database.

"When we compared what I uncovered from my search of obituaries with the database that Nolan hacked into, we found a remarkable coincidence between those entries that had been designated with peculiar highlighted '**.htl**' extensions on their files and those faculty members who had died under suspicious circumstances. The correspondence between the two cannot be fortuitous. But I have to admit that all the evidence we have discovered is purely circumstantial and could never stand up to the scrutiny of an intensive investigation. Frankly, I know I'm right about these contrived deaths, but I'm stymied as to what to do next. I just wanted to let you know that I'm not going to give up. I plan to continue my inquiry into these deaths. I realize I may never be able to uncover the truth and bring those bastards who are responsible to justice; but, so help me God, it won't be because I didn't give it my best shot."

"Alex, I'm really concerned about your safety now. I think you're playing with fire and exposing yourself and Nolan to potential harm. You're liable to upset some very powerful people who have the wherewithal to arrange your death and that of Nolan as well. Why don't you just leave it alone before it's too late? You don't want to make a widow out of Victoria, do you?"

"Don't worry about Nolan. He assured me that there was no way to trace his hacking of Noble's database back to him. Besides, he's out of the picture now because I have asked him to send a copy of the database files to me. Hopefully he will delete his copy of the files. I won't be asking him for any more help. I'll keep you posted. Please give my best to Marylyn."

"Just be careful, Alex. Goodbye."

CHAPTER 14: SURVEILLED

It was several days before Marty McIver checked Chris's cellphone calls at Noble Computing's security center. For the past several months there had been so little activity on Chris's cell phone that Noble's monitoring system had been modified to record only long distance phone calls received or sent by Chris. After Marty listened to the conversation between Alex and Chris in which Nolan Martin's name was linked to the hacking incident, he immediately alerted Roger Anderson, head of the AAPS Division.

"Roger, this is Marty. Could you please come to the security central office and listen to a conversation we recorded between Chris Carpenter, whom we have been monitoring, and somebody named Alex, who has disclosed the name of the person responsible for our hacking incident."

"I'll be right there. Maybe we can finally get to the bottom of all this and find out what the hell is going on."

After a few minutes, Roger entered the room, placed a headset over his ears, and listened intently. He heard Alex disclose that someone named Nolan Martin had breached AAPS's security system and was sending all the data that he had downloaded to Alex. Roger wondered out loud, "Who in the hell is this guy Alex, and who is his contact Nolan Martin? Maybe Malcolm will have an idea about who these people are."

Before disclosing what he had found out to Malcolm, Roger recalled that Alex had referred to Nolan Martin as an old fraternity brother. Roger also suspected that Chris and Alex were connected from their college days, and knowing from his earlier search of the database that Chris had attended Ashmore, he began a search of all those students named Alex who were there at the same time as Chris. It became apparent from his data search, that the most likely Alex who had attended Ashmore at the same time that Chris was there was Alex Chandler. He also noted in a recent Ashmore alumni newsletter that there had been a class reunion recently in which both Chris and Alex were listed as attendees. As Roger scanned the list of reunion attendees, he noticed that Nolan Martin had also attended the event.

"Obviously, all three of these guys are somehow linked, and not just by all having attended Ashmore. I don't know what they're up to, but we sure as hell have to find out. We can't afford to have anybody nosing around in our business at this time. We have to nip this in the bud. I'll check with Malcolm and see if he has any information about either Nolan Martin or this Alex Chandler. Alert our surveillance team that we may have some business for them to attend to."

Roger went online and in fairly short order was able to determine that Nolan lived in Miami and that Alex lived in Hilton Head. Roger then downloaded a copy of the conversation between Alex and Chris on a handheld digital recorder and headed to Malcolm's office, which was located in a private suite on the top floor of Noble Cloud Computing's corporate headquarters. He asked Malcolm's administrative assistant, Janice, if he was available.

"I'll check, Roger. You know that he hasn't been feeling well lately. I think it's the chemo."

"Yes, I know. I wouldn't bother him if it weren't very important."

Janice returned in a few minutes and indicated that Malcolm would see him. "Please, try not to stress him out. He's been resting."

"I'll do my best. Thanks, Janice."

Malcolm was seated behind a massive desk that was blanketed with piles of papers in such a haphazard manner that the desk's surface was totally obscured.

"Come in, Roger. Have a seat. Now tell me what's on your mind that is so important."

"Malcolm, I think you need to hear this recording of a conversation between Dr. Chris Carpenter, who you may recall visited us a few months back, and a Dr. Alex Chandler."

Malcolm listened intently until he heard the name Nolan Martin mentioned. Then he blurted out, "Well, that son of a bitch!"

"So you know who this Nolan Martin is?"

"You're damn right I do! A few years ago we bought his company, Martin Security Services, for several million dollars. So he is the one responsible for breaching our security system. Why on earth would he do that?"

"If you listen to the rest of the recording, I think his motive will be apparent."

Malcom became more agitated as the recording continued.

"Turn it off! I've heard enough. It looks as though Alex Chandler is the one ultimately responsible for prying into our business and it appears that he persuaded his old friend to help him probe deeper into our operation. We'll have to deal with both of them. The first order of business is to remove any records that were hacked from our AAPS database that still reside on Nolan Martin's computer and server. He obviously still has significant computational power at his disposal. Check out our database to see where Martin lives and if he is operating out of a rented office or out of his home. I think we need to move on this as soon as possible. Roger, can I count on you to take care of this ASAP? After we've taken care of this Nolan Martin matter, we'll focus on this Alex Chandler fellow. He seems to be the one that we should be most concerned about and who apparently is the one driving this whole intrusion into our operation."

"Don't worry, sir. I'll get on this right away."

"See that you do… and keep me posted. I'll expect an update from you within the next few days."

Roger nodded affirmatively and left Malcolm's office. It wasn't too difficult to locate Nolan Martin's home address in Coral Gables, Florida. There appeared to be no record of any office space currently rented to Martin, so Roger assumed he was likely operating out of his home. Roger alerted his security team that they had an assignment in south Florida and that they should be prepared for rapid deployment as the matter they would deal with was of great concern to Malcolm.

As Roger continued to prepare a dossier on Nolan Martin, he found that Nolan had divorced his first and only wife. She had retained custody of their three children and had relocated to Tampa to be near her parents who had retired there, weary of the dreary winter weather in Columbus, Ohio. Nolan's sale of his company to Noble Computing apparently afforded him a very luxurious lifestyle. Nolan now lived in an upscale neighborhood in Coral Gables off Old Cutler Road in a Spanish-style house with a white stucco exterior, a red tile roof, a swimming pool, and a four-car garage. The house was surrounded by a lush growth of tropical plants highlighted by several large palm trees. Two slots in the garage were occupied by vintage Ferraris that had been restored to their original glory. The other slots in the garage were occupied by his eighteen-foot Boston Whaler and a bright, yellow Humvee that he used for his daily commute to Dinner Key Marina in Coconut Grove where he kept his forty-foot sloop moored.

The surveillance crew of four led by Jason Palmer was in place in Coral Gables within a few days. Jason had had extensive experience in black operations in Afghanistan. His covert activities included surveillance, kidnapping, and in a few instances, assassinations. His demeanor was always somber, and the stone-cold look in his eyes instilled fear in any combatant who was unfortunate enough to be held his captive. If ever in a tight spot, you would want someone like Jason on your team. His often brutal interrogation techniques were largely responsible for his being barred from any further action in Afghanistan and being shipped back to the United States, where he found work in private security services. The other three accomplices were assigned to monitor Nolan Martin's daily activities and to determine when the best time would be to avoid detection when entering Nolan's residence. Also an expert at disarming computer systems, Jason would be the one responsible for entering Nolan's house to determine if his computing equipment contained the records that had been hacked from Noble Computing's database.

The house next door to Nolan was up for sale and vacant. A local realtor was having an open house that conveniently allowed access not only to potential buyers, but also to the surveillance crew posing as interested buyers. While serious buyers were examining the house, one of the crew surreptitiously installed two small cameras in the windows facing Nolan's house so that his comings and goings could be monitored remotely. Once the cameras were in place, Nolan could be monitored from afar from their van that was disguised as a cable TV repair truck.

There would be little chance that he would know that he was being surveilled.

Over the next few days, it became apparent that Nolan was a creature of habit. After a jog in the morning, followed by brief shower, Nolan would drive to a small coffee shop in Coconut Grove where he would meet a small group of his sailing friends for lunch. Afterwards, if the weather was clear and the winds favorable, he would spend the afternoon sailing on Biscayne Bay, usually with a woman companion, but not necessarily the same one every day. Often Nolan would anchor the boat, don his flippers, facemask, and snorkel, and scour the rocky outcrops or patch reefs for the telltale antennae of Florida crayfish hiding in the crevices. Little did he know that his every move was being watched from a boat that was anchored nearby.

After a few days, the surveillance crew, now reasonably confident that Nolan's routine was predictable, decided that two men would follow him the next day as he sailed Biscayne Bay and keep Jason informed as to his whereabouts at all times. Jason would enter Nolan's house from the side facing the vacant property next door. His remaining partner would man the cable truck parked outside the vacant house while pretending to service the cable connection on the nearby telephone pole.

Right on schedule, the next afternoon Nolan drove off in his Humvee for his sailing ritual, followed by the surveillance crew that would continue to monitor his activities. Once Nolan's sailboat left its mooring and was sailing in the open waters of Biscayne Bay, Jason was given the go-ahead to break into Nolan's house. Jason's partner pulled the cable truck decoy into the driveway of the vacant house. He scaled the telephone pole out front pretending to examine the cable box while Jason disabled the alarm box on Nolan's house and entered through the sliding glass doors adjacent to the swimming pool.

After a brief tour of the entire house, Jason found Nolan's home office to be outfitted with state-of-the-art computers and peripherals, including a powerful server. Jason powered up the main computer that was connected to the server and without much difficulty was able to hack Nolan's password and scan the contents of the computer's hard drives as well as the server. It took nearly twenty minutes to scroll through the massive amount of data stored on the server, but Jason succeeded in finding the files that had been compromised and stolen from the AAPS database. These data were not found on the computer hard drives, but only stored on the server. Rather than risk detection by taking the time to disable the server, Jason decided to simply disconnect the server and take it with him as he exited the house. After reconnecting the alarm system, he notified his partner to return to the van where he would join him so they could make their escape, hopefully without arousing any suspicion or detection by the neighbors. The entire operation went as smoothly and as successfully as could be hoped for.

Now that the incriminating evidence had been removed, Nolan posed little threat to Noble Computing. It was assumed that when Nolan discovered that his server had been stolen, he would realize that his hacking activity likely had been detected and that any further action on his part might bring more serious retribution from Noble. As the cable truck left Nolan's house, Jason contacted the other two men who were tailing Nolan in Biscayne

Bay to let them know they could return to the marina and that the operation had been a success.

Jason then called Roger at Noble Computing's headquarters.

"Roger. This is Jason. Just wanted you to know that everything went smoothly and that I have in my possession all the relevant data that were copied from our computers. I'm sure when Nolan returns to his house and finds his server missing, he will put two and two together and realize that he probably just dodged a bullet. I suspect he will be in touch with whomever he sent these data to and that person should be our next objective. Perhaps both Nolan and he will have to be dealt with more severely. But of course, that will be up to you and Malcolm. I'm flying back to Atlanta this evening. I'll be back in the office tomorrow morning to discuss with you what our next move should be."

"Jason, that's good news. Are you absolutely sure you have removed all the files that he hacked from us and that he doesn't pose any further danger to our operation?"

"Absolutely. I scanned every drive on his computer and the only external data storage device that he had connected to the computer. The server that I retrieved was the only device that contained the information we were looking for. I think we can rest assured that he is no longer a threat. We will continue to monitor his phone calls and emails to see how he reacts to the loss of his server and if he contacts anyone about it being stolen. See you tomorrow."

Roger hung up the telephone, leaned back in his chair with a broad smile on his face, realizing now that he had good news to relay to Malcolm, who was still very much upset about the breach in Noble Computing's security.

Malcolm was delighted with the news and decided that he would place a call to Nolan Martin after he was reasonably certain that Nolan had detected the loss of his server. He instructed Roger to thoroughly search through all the information contained on Nolan's server in order to determine if other information had been stored that might possibly link Nolan to any other scandalous activities that could possibly be used against him should he disclose the robbery to the authorities.

CHAPTER 15: CONFRONTATION

When Nolan Martin returned to his house he attempted to check on the performance of his stock portfolio and soon discovered that his server had been stolen. It was clear to him that this burglary was not random, but focused on the server that contained a significant amount of information that could incriminate him if it were ever made public. In some cases, these files could potentially put his life in danger. He pondered all the information that he had stored on the server and began to wonder who felt so threatened that they would take this action against him. Could it be an angry spouse of one of the women with whom he had had secret trysts? Could it be more seriously the drug cartel with which he had conducted some illicit business? Or could it be any number of files that potentially he could use against others for political favors? He assumed that eventually whoever was responsible for the thievery would contact him in one way or another. It was several sleepless nights before he finally received his answer when he was awakened in the dead of the night by the telephone resting on the nightstand by his bedside.

"Hello, Nolan. Sorry to awaken you at this ungodly hour, but I think it's time you and I had a heartfelt conversation. Perhaps you recognize my voice; and then again, perhaps you don't. I'm sure you'll remember me when I tell you that I'm the man responsible for making you a multimillionaire."

"Yes, Malcolm, I recognize your voice," said Nolan, still groggy from being awakened so abruptly. "I was beginning to wonder who might be responsible for stealing the server from my house. In a way, I must say I'm a bit relieved. I'm sure you saw that all I removed from your server were the files of the faculty stored in your AAPS database. I did so for an old friend who was just curious and wanted to compile some data on faculty demographics. I admit that I should've contacted you directly and asked for your permission to do so, but I considered my attempt to hack into your database a challenge."

"Nolan, you and I both know that's bullshit! Let me assure you that operations we have underway will in no way be jeopardized by you or your compatriot, whatever your motives may be. Let me tell you how this is going to play out. We have scrutinized the entire contents of your server. We have detected several irregularities in your stock transactions that I'm sure would be of interest to the SEC. We know about your offshore accounts and the potential tax consequences if they are disclosed to the IRS. From your email messages, we know about the trysts you have had with married women and know the names of their unsuspecting spouses. In essence we know far more about you than anyone would ever want to know. You realize that you have ventured into dangerous territory and that your intrusion into our activities could have had dire consequences for you. Let's just say we will hang on to all your files and suggest that you distance yourself from any further activity relative to Noble Computing or its AAPS program."

"Are you threatening me?"

"Is this a threat? You bet your ass it is! And I assure you that we will continue to monitor your activities to see that you comply with my demands. There are only two possible outcomes should you choose to ignore my request. One is the disclosure of all the illegal and unsavory information that we have discovered about you. Our second option is to simply remove you from the equation. Do I make myself clear, Nolan? I don't want your name to ever cross my desk again for I assure you the consequences will be dire. Have a good night, Nolan."

Nolan sat on the edge of his bed, trembling, realizing now that he never should have gotten involved with Alex and his probing into AAPS activities. He realized that he had not heard Malcolm mention Alex's name. Perhaps they had not discovered with whom he had been conspiring. Unable to fall asleep after that disturbing call from Malcolm, Nolan spent the rest of the night nervously awaiting the morning so that he could call Alex and alert him of what had transpired. Perhaps if Alex stopped his probing into AAPS affairs, he might not be discovered and could avoid the wrath of Malcolm in whatever form that might take. On the other hand, if Alex's link to Nolan was already known to Malcolm, alerting Alex to that possibility was paramount. It was mid-morning before Nolan decided to call Alex's home phone. It was several moments before he answered.

"Alex here. Who's calling please?"

"Alex, this is Nolan. I'm afraid I have some very bad news. I received a call last night from Malcolm Fowler, Noble Computing's president, who raised hell with me about hacking into his database. His people broke into my house and stole the server that contained all of the information that I downloaded from the AAPS database. The server also contained a lot of unsavory information about me that they were able to retrieve, and he threatened to use it against me if I didn't keep my mouth shut. I don't know if they have as yet been able to connect the two of us, but I think I should warn you that it likely is only a matter of time before they do. Malcolm clearly indicated to me that my life could be in danger if I continued probing into their affairs. I'm sure the same would apply to you... perhaps even more so for you as you are actively pursuing leads from that list. It is in your best interest to back off, Alex. These guys are deadly serious. They won't hesitate to eliminate you if you get in their way. As you already know, they are very proficient at orchestrating "accidental deaths." I don't think I'm overreacting when I say that I have to distance myself from you and any further involvement in your investigation. I still don't know how Noble was able to link me with the hacking of their database."

Alex was dumbfounded by what Nolan had told him and conflicted in his emotions. He now was acutely aware of the potential threat to his own life posed by Malcolm and felt a fear far greater than any he had ever experienced. He was deeply distressed at having put Nolan in danger by asking him for help. He realized now that it was unlikely that he ever could discover what the real motives were behind the mysterious deaths that he had been investigating and questioned his own judgment for ignoring how serious the potential consequences could be for his actions.

"Nolan, I'm really sorry that I put you in such a bad position. I admit that I may be the one responsible for Malcolm learning your identity. In my conversations with Chris I was always very careful not to mention your name … except for once when I inadvertently mentioned your name thinking that Chris's cell phone was secure. Apparently I was mistaken. They probably know my identity as well, and I can expect some kind of retaliation from them. Please avoid any further contact with me and accept my sincerest apologies for getting you into this mess. I never should've gotten you involved in this. I feel terrible that I put you in such danger."

"Alex, don't worry about me. I knew what the risk was all along. I guess I overestimated my ability to avoid detection and underestimated their ability to track me down. Based on what Malcolm said to me, I don't think I'm in any further danger so long as I don't meddle in his affairs. But that's not to say that you don't have to watch your back. Perhaps nothing will come of it now that I have been exposed, but please keep a low profile... at least until things cool down. Better still, drop the whole investigation and get on with your life. Perhaps I'll see you again at the next reunion, but until then I won't be in touch. Goodbye."

It was hard to absorb all that Nolan had just disclosed to him. The possibility of his own life being in danger, perhaps even Victoria's, distressed him to the point that he doubled over in pain. "My God, what have I gotten myself into?" he uttered out loud. He felt helpless and personally threatened for the first time since his investigation had begun. He was only now beginning to realize the gravity of the situation he had created. Could he extricate himself from his obsession in time to avoid retribution from Malcolm and his cohorts, whoever they were? He would soon learn that the die already had been cast.

CHAPTER 16: WORST FEARS REALIZED

Alex didn't say anything to Victoria, as he didn't want to upset her. But he was genuinely concerned about his safety after his conversation with Nolan. Would Malcolm and his henchmen make an overt attempt to silence him? Nolan's warning was not taken lightly by Alex, and he decided that it was prudent not to pursue the matter further. He assumed that Noble would monitor his activities further to determine if he still posed a threat to their criminal mission. He reasoned that if he would just lay low, perhaps they would leave him be. On the other hand, perhaps Malcolm was not going to be satisfied unless somehow Alex paid for the disruption that he had caused. Alex had no way of judging just how vindictive someone like Malcolm could be, but he believed him to be culpable in multiple murders. There was little else that Alex could do other than wait and see what transpired now that the "cat was clearly out of the bag."

Victoria sensed that Alex was not himself over the next week. He seemed tense and irritated whenever she attempted to ask him what was wrong. He began to retreat into himself and spent more time than usual jogging and fishing from the local pier. It was clear that Alex wanted to be left alone and was so deeply troubled by something that solitude was his only recourse. It wouldn't take long before the solitude would be broken in a very dramatic way.

Victoria was particularly disturbed about Alex's demeanor as she had planned to be out of the country the following week. A short time after they moved to Hilton Head, she and a friend opened a small curio shop catering to the more affluent clientele of Hilton Head. Their shop specialized in unique household items that were available in Europe but not found in most US retail stores. It was now late January, and they had planned a trip to London and Paris to scour the stores for new items that could attract their regular customers in addition to the tourists who frequent the island during the summer season. Victoria questioned whether or not it was advisable to leave Alex alone in his present state of mind. She discussed this with Alex who assured her that he would be fine and that she should not cancel her trip. This was a late winter ritual that seemed to revitalize Victoria and increase her enthusiasm for their shop. Reluctantly, she decided to go ahead and make the trip and, within a few days, was on her way to Europe.

Despite the dire warning that Nolan had given Alex to cease his obsession or risk life-threatening retribution from Noble Computing, Alex persisted in searching the Internet, not on his home computer, but at the library and other Wi-Fi hotspots at local coffee shops. He continued to find numerous suspicious instances of deaths of elderly tenured professors – professors whose names appeared on the AAPS list that Nolan had sent him and which contained the distinctive ".**htl**" extension in bold face type. His frustration only intensified because he knew that, despite all his efforts, he could never prove that there was a link between AAPS and these deaths. Alex felt reasonably confident that his Internet searches were secure and not detectable by those who might wish him harm for his persistence. Sadly, he was mistaken.

The same surveillance crew that had monitored Nolan's activities was already in place in Hilton Head under the guise of a private security patrol orchestrated by one of Malcolm's board members who had a summer home on Hilton Head. Unknown to Alex, his and Victoria's every move had been watched ever since he received the call from Nolan. This surveillance included his visits to the library as well as to Wi-Fi hotspots. As before, Jason was in charge and was deciding what strategy would be best to implement the instructions given to him by Malcolm. The discovery that Victoria had left for Europe provided an ideal opportunity to initiate an abduction plan.

Alex and Victoria's home was located in the Hilton Head Plantation development, an upscale, gated community comprising nearly four thousand acres bounded on one side by Port Royal Sound and on the other by the Intracoastal Waterway. Alex particularly enjoyed his homesite that bordered the Waterway where he spent countless hours watching boats ranging from large yachts to small dinghies come and go. The numerous trails and boardwalks running through woods and marshes that were maintained and protected by the Nature Conservancy were favorite pathways for Alex's morning jogs.

Unbeknownst to Alex, Jason had jogged at a safe distance behind Alex for several days to survey the layout of the trail that he frequented so that he could determine the best place to abduct him without detection. Finally a decision was reached as to the day and the time for the abduction. On the appointed day, aware of the route that Alex would take on his morning jog, Jason placed one of his men ahead of Alex and one behind him. When they were reasonably sure that no other runners were on the trail between them and Alex, they closed the gap. The runner in front of Alex feigned a sprained ankle and slowed down while the other sped up his running until Alex was only a short distance in front of him. When Alex slowed down to see if he could help the limping runner, he was subdued by the runner from behind who injected Alex with a strong sedative. Within minutes he was rendered unconscious. A van had been placed strategically nearby, and within moments Alex was whisked away.

It was several hours before Alex regained consciousness, still groggy from the sedative. He found himself lying on the floor in the back of the van, still in running clothes, hands and feet bound, gagged, and blindfolded. He began to hear bits and pieces of a conversation going on between the driver and his accomplices. He listened intently to what they were saying, especially whenever he heard Nolan's name mentioned.

"That was a pretty clever way they dealt with Nolan. I can't believe that he thought he would be allowed to get away with hacking into our computers with just a warning and a slap on the wrist. Whose idea was it to use stonefish venom to kill him?"

"That was my idea," replied Jason. "I knew there was a lionfish invasion that has been spreading from Florida to the Carolinas. Toxin from the lionfish generally only causes throbbing pain that can last for hours, but it also can cause abnormal heart rhythms, seizures, decreased blood pressure and even death. While Nolan was diving for lobsters, he was so preoccupied that he didn't notice our diver approaching him from behind. A high dose of concentrated lionfish venom was injected into his neck. Nolan writhed in pain briefly before paralysis set in. He drowned within minutes."

Hearing that Nolan had been murdered for his part in Alex's investigation, his own worst fears were now being realized. Would he suffer a similar fate under some contrived accidental death? His thoughts turned to Victoria and how she would cope with his loss. He thought of his children and the grandchildren. He realized that he was in over his head to a much greater extent than he had ever imagined and that his quest for justice was clearly a foolhardy exercise that now could lead to his untimely death. Gripped with fear, his heart racing as beads of sweat trickled down his forehead, Alex felt helpless in the grasp of his captors. Alex moaned and thought, *Dear God, what have I done?*

CHAPTER 17: RETRIBUTION

The van continued for what seemed like an eternity at a very high rate of speed, likely on an interstate highway, thought Alex, before it finally slowed down and turned off the highway. After traveling a few miles on a gravel road, the van came to an abrupt stop. He could hear a muffled conversation between the men as they left the van and slammed the doors. He waited in anticipation for the rear door to be opened, but it never was. He could hear the voices of his abductors fading as they walked away. Alex lay in excruciating silence for what seemed like another hour or so not knowing where he was nor what his fate would be.

At last he could hear the crunching of gravel as someone approached the rear door of the van and flung it open. The ropes that bound his feet were removed so that he could walk. The blindfold and gag remained in place as did his hand restraints. Two men, one on each side, said nothing as they dragged Alex, still feeling the effects of the sedative, across the gravel lot until he felt a solid surface beneath his feet. Within a few minutes, another vehicle approached and came to a stop.

"Put him in the back. I'll take it from here."

Alex was shoved headfirst into the back seat of a car. He could hear the automatic door locks snap shut as the car sped away. Within a few minutes, the car slowed down and stopped. With the engine still running, the driver left the car. Shortly thereafter, Alex heard what he perceived to be a large, rolling steel door being opened. The driver returned, drove a short distance, and turned off the engine. Alex could hear the door closing and assumed that he was now inside some sort of building, but what kind and where? Unbeknownst to Alex, he was now in the expansive interior loading bay of Noble Computing.

The car door was opened and Alex was forcefully dragged out of the back seat. Unable to regain his balance, he stumbled and fell to the concrete floor.

"Stand up, you lucky son of a bitch," said Jason. "Someone wants to have words with you."

Alex couldn't help but wonder how anyone in his situation could be considered "lucky".

The struggle to walk continued for several minutes until they paused to climb a short flight of concrete stairs. Then Alex heard what he thought was an elevator door being opened, and was pushed inside. The elevator slowly climbed several floors before it came to an abrupt stop. As the doors opened, Alex was shoved forward onto a soft surface that felt like plush carpeting. After a few steps, they stopped and Alex heard knocking on a door.

"Enter," came the reply.

A rush of cool air struck Alex in the face as the door opened.

"Put him down in that chair," said a voice unfamiliar to Alex. "Remove the gag and blindfold and free his hands. Wait outside the door until I call for you."

"As you wish. Anything else, sir?"

"No. That will be all for now. Thank you, Jason, for another job well done."

Alex rubbed his eyes after the blindfold was removed and saw that he was seated at the end of a long conference table in an expansive paneled conference room that was lined with several large portraits. At the other end of the table was a wheelchair with its back facing him.

"What the hell is going on here? Where am I? Why have I been brought here? What are you planning to do with me? And who the hell are you anyway?"

The wheelchair slowly turned around to reveal a frail, elderly man with thinning white hair, breathing oxygen from a tank that was anchored to his wheelchair. His breathing was labored, and it was obviously difficult for him to speak.

"Welcome to Noble Computing, or shall I say, Academic Appointment Placement Services, or AAPS as you call it. Try to relax, Dr. Chandler. You are in no danger here as you will learn that my misfortune has become your good fortune. Unfortunately, the same cannot be said for your friend, Nolan Martin. His betrayal was abhorrent to me after all I did for him. I wasn't about to allow him to get off scot-free.

"I have known for some time that you have been investigating our activities and discussing them with your colleague, Dr. Chris Carpenter. We accessed your computer some time ago and have been monitoring all your emails and website searches, including all the obituaries that have so intrigued you and continued to arouse your suspicions. I might add that Dr. Carpenter is not in danger. Rather than assisting you, he tried vigorously to dissuade you from pursuing your investigation further. It would have been better for all, especially Nolan, if you had heeded his warning.

"You deserve a little background and perhaps a rationale for what you have uncovered. My name is Malcolm Fowler, and I am the founder and owner of Noble Computing. I come from a very privileged family. My great-grandfather founded a very successful chemical company that specialized in supplying chemical additives for a wide variety of plastic products. After his death, my father took over the leadership of the company and broadened its capabilities to include other industries. It was clear that it was his intention that I too would take over the company ultimately; but, to his dismay, I had no interest in doing so.

"I began my undergraduate education at Harvard, majoring in chemistry as my father had wished. I continued my education as a graduate student at Caltech earning both a master's degree and a PhD. As part of my training, I assisted in one of the elementary laboratories as a teaching assistant. I realized from that experience that what I really wanted out of life was to be a teacher. Consequently, rather than returning to the chemical industry as my father had wished, I accepted a tenure track teaching position as an assistant professor at one of the Ivy League schools, which shall go unnamed. I was regarded as an excellent teacher by my students and actually won an undergraduate teaching award for my introductory course in inorganic chemistry. I published several articles in prestigious chemical journals, gave presentations at national meetings, served on several university committees, and believed that I was well on my way toward a tenured appointment. When the time came for a tenure review committee to evaluate my teaching, research, university service, and grant procurement, I was shocked to learn that I had been denied tenure. It was a devastating blow to my psyche. I wondered why I had not been awarded tenure as I had done everything necessary to deserve it. I was told I was a little light on my publication record and that my research interests were too broad with little potential for new insights into chemical research. I was extremely angered by the decision of the senior faculty, many of whom in my opinion were far less qualified than I, both with regard to teaching and research. I left the university feeling cheated, vindictive, and determined to someday do something about a system that I felt was faulty.

"I returned to the family company with my tail between my legs, so to speak. For years I slowly worked my way up the ladder until, upon my father's death, I became president and owner of the company. By then we were a Fortune 500 Company worth billions of dollars. After receiving a most generous offer from a competing chemical company, I decided to sell. For several years I contemplated how I should spend my time and my money. I was intrigued by the emerging field of computer applications, and though I knew very little about it, I had the wherewithal to surround myself with knowledgeable people and founded Noble Computing.

"You see the portraits of these twelve gentlemen lining the walls of this boardroom. These men were handpicked by me for their expertise in computational science, mathematics, statistics, and finance. They are all experts in their fields, and all have had teaching experience at the university level.

"They also have one other important attribute in common—all of them were denied tenure at the institutions where they taught. They all felt that they were treated unfairly. They all share my disdain for the tenure process in general and what it has become—a system that permits those having been granted tenure the freedom to continue teaching and research, or the lack thereof, with no further formal performance review that could warrant their dismissal. The resistance of older tenured faculty to retire precludes an infusion of younger, better prepared, often more enthusiastic teachers to the detriment of the entire educational system. I firmly believe that tenure will no longer exist in our universities within a decade. It will be supplanted by a system that insists on continued performance at a high level for all faculty members, regardless of age. There will no longer be a place for those aging faculty who are coasting into retirement while contributing relatively little to the academic enterprise.

"In the meantime, so long as the present system persists and young, aspiring doctoral students are denied an opportunity because older faculty members are refusing to retire, I decided to do something about it. My goal, so to speak, was to effectively prune the academic tree, getting rid of the deadwood while encouraging new branches to sprout and bring renewed life and vitality to the tree. From our extensive database, I screened fifty actively-teaching, tenured professors seventy years or older who were producing very little published research as of late and whose teaching ability was characterized as poor, based on their course evaluations and subsequent comments on our crowdsourcing website. I designated those that I felt needed to be reviewed by the board with the '.htl' extension."

"I'm curious, what was the meaning of the '.htl' extension? Was it an acronym of some sort?" asked Alex.

Malcolm smiled, or rather smirked, and said, "No, it was only an abbreviated form that I chose for those that I placed on my 'hit list.' I submitted a dossier to every member of my board for each of the fifty faculty members that I had selected for possible elimination. The names of the selected faculty were not included, nor were their institutional affiliations. They were simply assigned random numbers, and I was the only one who held the key to their true identities.

"I asked board members to review each resumé and assign a value-order ranking for each candidate; a value ranking of one indicating the lowest level of value and ten the highest. After all the responses were reviewed and tabulated, the lowest rated group of twenty professors was selected, and highlighted in the data base with the bold '.htl'extensions. Only I knew the identity of the actual faculty members selected by the collective evaluation of the board members.

"My first approach, which I shared with my board members, was to contact each of these faculty members with a letter from a fictitious academic employment agency saying that an anonymous donor, in order to provide opportunities for newly minted PhD candidates, was willing to offer them an incentive of $250,000 to relinquish tenure and retire.

Two of those contacted accepted my offer and were paid from an offshore account after they retired. The other eighteen declined the offer and chose to continue as active faculty members.

"It became apparent to me at that time that I had to take another approach to resolve this matter. I did so entirely on my own, not disclosing to the members of my board that what I was about to do was illegal, immoral, heartless, and done without remorse. I conspired with black operatives and unscrupulous hit men to create accidental-appearing circumstances whereby the remaining academic holdouts would be eliminated. Dr. Chandler, it may interest you to know that among the accidental cases that you investigated only fourteen of those were in fact instigated by me. I'm sorry to say that your friend and Ashmore colleague, Dr. Paul Armstrong, was one so designated. The others, however, died of natural causes, including Dr. Parker Johnson. I know you felt we were complicit in his death on the tram in New Mexico, but he suffered a fatal heart attack from natural causes. He had a history of cardiac events that perhaps you were not aware of. The fact that you are still alive today is only because you never attempted to make your findings and suspicions public. Had we suspected you were about to do so, I can assure you that you wouldn't be present for our discussion today.

"I alone am responsible for taking these actions and upon my death surely will answer to my maker. I will disavow all of my board members of any responsibility for these murders. I'm confident that you cannot possibly comprehend what drove me to take such drastic actions. I would like to think that my motives were purely altruistic, but I know they were primarily driven by revenge and rage. I actually was so distraught when I was denied tenure, that I arranged for the murder of one of the faculty members that I considered most responsible for the emotional distress that I still suffer to this very day. Once I crossed over that bridge, it wasn't very difficult to justify, in my mind at least, the killing of others to satisfy my anger, irrational as it might be."

Malcolm's voice was growing weaker by the minute, and his breathing was becoming more labored.

"As you can see, I am not in good health. I suffer from terminal cancer believed to have been caused through contact with toxic chemicals while investigating a spill at one of our chemical plants many years ago. The doctors tell me that I only have a very short time to live, perhaps only days. Upon my death, documents and a confessional video I have prepared will be released to the news media disclosing what I have done and what drove me to do so. As I said, I will absolve my board members from any involvement in the heinous activities orchestrated by me, although a few of them were actually involved in planning the murders. Each of my four assassins will be provided with a new identity and will be handsomely compensated with a sizable offshore account. It is very unlikely that any of them will ever be linked to me and brought to justice. I assure you that no one else in our organization will continue along the path that I followed.

"I have instructed the board to continue our stated mission to place recent graduates in academic institutions using our AAPS program. To that end, I have created a 500 million dollar trust fund constructed to offer assistance to recent graduates who are steeped in debt; these funds will give them a fresh start. The $250,000 inducement offer to relinquish tenure and retire will be advertised nationally to encourage other senior faculty over the age of seventy to consider retirement. Perhaps in some small way, despite the diabolical manner in which I attempted to do so, I may encourage further review of the value and manner in which tenure is administered."

Malcolm slowly slumped in his wheel chair, his voice trailed off, his head twisted downward at an awkward angle, as Alex heard what he perceived to be Malcolm's last breath. Alex rose from his chair, rushed to the door, and summoned Jason who was waiting outside. Jason rushed to Malcolm's side and shook him vigorously, attempting to arouse him but to no avail. He dialed 911 on his cell phone, but it was obvious that Malcolm had breathed his last breath. He was gone.

Alex sat in a chair opposite the lifeless body of Malcolm while awaiting the arrival of paramedics who would be able to do nothing more than confirm that he had died. There would be no justice for Malcolm's victims other than perhaps some closure for those who had suffered the loss of a loved one. As Alex sat there he wondered how someone could be so devastated by being denied tenure by his colleagues so many years before that he would resort to such extreme measures to attempt to satisfy his insatiable desire for vengeance. With all the financial resources that Malcolm had at his command, couldn't he have found a more humane way to channel his hatred and anger without resorting to murder? There are many other former faculty members who have experienced tenure rejection that was just as devastating as his. Most of them simply moved on with their lives, burdened by a psychological wound that may never completely heal.

The medics arrived in short order and, despite Herculean efforts to revive Malcolm, pronounced him dead at the scene. Alex sat in silence as the paramedics removed Malcolm's lifeless body. His thoughts turned to his own well-being now that Malcolm had died. Would he still be considered a threat to AAPS, and if so, what was to be his fate?

Alex was relieved when Jason reentered the room and told him that he was free to go and that he would be escorted back to Hilton Head, but not without a chilling declaration from Jason.

"You'll never know how close you came to death. If Malcolm had lived another month, you wouldn't still be alive. We were becoming increasingly annoyed by your persistence and decided that you had to be dealt with just in case you decided to go public with your suspicions before Malcolm had an opportunity to alert the media on his own terms. The rapid deterioration of his health saved your ass. He called me just after we left Hilton Head, with you in the van. We had already decided how we would dispose of your body, but Malcolm instructed me to bring you to Atlanta instead. You're one lucky son of a bitch, Dr. Chandler."

CHAPTER 18: DELIVERANCE

Jason accompanied Alex to a limousine waiting outside the main entrance to Noble Computing and instructed the driver to take Alex to the private hangar where Noble's corporate jets were housed. Alex was ushered into one of the smaller jets and instructed to buckle up. Within minutes, the two jet engines sprang to life, and soon they were taxiing down the runway for takeoff.

Alex sat alone in the passenger portion of the jet, staring out of the window as the plane became airborne. He became lost in his thoughts as he reflected on what had just transpired. Jason's comment that he was only spared because Malcolm's death came earlier than the doctor's predictions made him realize the significance of what Malcolm had meant when he said that his misfortune was Alex's good fortune. But was Malcolm's reassurance that Alex had nothing to fear actually true, or were there plans already in place that might still result in his death? He chose not to dwell on that possibility and decided to take Malcolm at his word that he was no longer in danger.

Realizing how close he had come to death was a terrifying experience for Alex. The realization that he was largely responsible for Nolan's death was devastating. He wished that he had listened to Chris and had not drawn Nolan into his dogged search for the truth about those deaths that had occurred under suspicious circumstances. He knew he could never forgive himself for Nolan's murder, and it would be something that he would regret for the rest of his life.

Alex would have much to share with Victoria when they were reunited.

It was difficult to come to grips with what Malcolm had just revealed to him in such a cold-blooded manner. He wondered if there was anything he could have done that might have stopped the bloodshed. He wondered whether anything would be accomplished once Malcolm's confession reached the news media. Would it give older faculty members pause, not for fear of retribution by someone as deranged as Malcolm, but driven by a moral obligation to retire and provide an opportunity for promising young scholars to take their places? Could academia survive with a tenure guarantee of indeterminate duration, or would tenure ultimately become a renewable contract based on evidence of continued excellence in research and teaching? Would a core of tenured faculty continue to be a vital part of institutional stability or would it become diminished as non-tenure track faculty and part-time instructors fill vacated positions? Would hiring be driven by budgetary constraints, so that part-time instructors and online courses would usurp the role of the traditional professor in the classroom?

It was obvious to Alex that there were no easy answers to these questions. He was convinced that the institutional structure that he had known as a tenured professor most likely would have to evolve into something quite different in the future.

The short plane ride from Atlanta ended abruptly as the private jet touched down on the tarmac at the small regional airport near Hilton Head. Alex exited the plane and entered the terminal, still dressed in his jogging clothes. Passengers awaiting their connecting flights paid little attention to Alex's attire and his lack of luggage. A curbside shuttle service provided transportation from the airport to Alex's home. Fortunately, Alex always carried his house keys and a small roll of bills when he jogged just in case of an emergency. He paid the driver and entered his vacant home, as Victoria would not be returning for another week.

Although exhausted from his kidnapping ordeal, Alex couldn't wait to take a hot shower and rid himself of his sweaty clothing. Afterwards, he was struck with a strong sense of loneliness and how empty the house felt now that Victoria was not there to welcome him home. With whom could he share his harrowing experience? He decided to call Chris and tell him of his traumatic kidnapping and his meeting with Malcolm at Noble computing.

After hearing everything that had happened to Alex and relieved that he was now safe at home, Chris said, "I think you're just damn lucky to still be alive. We can only hope that we will see some evidence soon that Malcolm's assurance of disclosure has actually been carried out. You don't know how relieved I am that this devastating ordeal is over for you. Stay in touch, old friend. Goodbye."

A few days passed and then the media coverage erupted with the story. The first to report the grizzly results of Malcolm's vengeful actions was Fox News followed in short order by the major television networks and widespread coverage in national newspapers. Malcolm's public disclosure gave Alex some comfort as he felt now there would be no further retribution as a result of his actions. Alex was relaxed in his easy chair, engrossed in reading a best-selling novel when the phone rang.

"Hello. Alex here. Who's calling?"

"Alex, it's Chris. I don't mean to alarm you, but I thought you should know about something that happened in Atlanta just a few days ago. Georgia Tech had arranged for a physics professor from Yale to give a seminar that I was planning to attend. The speaker was still an active member of the faculty although he was seventy-five years old. He was an accomplished pilot and planned to fly to Atlanta in his private plane. He had logged many thousand hours of flight time. For some unknown reason, his plane malfunctioned and he died in a fiery crash in North Georgia. It's probably just an unavoidable accident, but I hope that's all that it is. Perhaps, Alex, now I'm the one that's becoming paranoid. You did say that Malcolm assured you that his murdering spree was over, didn't he?"

"Yes, he did. I'm sure that the plane crash was an accident. Let's put this whole matter behind us and get on with our lives."

"I'm sure you're right Alex. My apologies. Let's just let sleeping dogs lie."

"Thanks for the call. Let's stay in touch."

"Will do."

Unfortunately, Chris's suspicion had reawaked the paranoia demons that haunted Alex's mind. It was difficult not to dwell on the trauma that he had experienced at the hands of Malcolm's henchmen and to wonder if there would be any further consequences for his actions. Aware that Victoria would be arriving home from her European travels in a few days, Alex spent considerable time contemplating how much of his ordeal he would share with her. Hopefully she would be grateful that he was still alive, but he also knew she would be angry that he had persisted in his relentless search for the truth and that his incessant actions had resulted in the death of a friend.

The next morning, Alex's curiosity got the best of him. He sat down with his laptop and began to search the Internet for newspaper accounts of the plane crash. He learned that the National Transportation Safety Board was examining the crash site, but as yet had not issued any statement concerning its investigation. Local residents who had observed the airplane in distress stated that they heard the engine sputtering as the plane lost altitude before crashing in a ball of fire.

Suddenly, without warning, Alex's screen began to flicker and fade to black. Efforts to restore the computer were futile. Then a chilling message in large block letters began to scroll across the screen:

THIS IS MY FINAL WARNING, DR. CHANDLER

DESIST OR DIE! . . . . JASON

The message then slowly faded and Alex's home page gradually reappeared. Beads of sweat trickled down Alex's brow as he shut down his laptop and breathed a huge sigh of relief. Despite Malcolm's assurance that his heinous activities would cease, perhaps there were still some wheels in motion that couldn't be stopped. Alex wondered how long he would continue to be monitored. Would he still be susceptible to retribution if any of his activities were perceived by Jason to be threatening, even if they weren't? It was evident that Alex had to distance himself from any further inquiries into suspicious deaths and be content knowing that he had survived a close brush with death. The ominous message from Jason was abundantly clear.... life or death. So far as Alex was concerned, the choice was obvious. He turned off his computer, poured himself a stiff drink, sat in darkness, and reflected on everything that had happened.

He decided that Victoria would never be told the whole story. After all, what purpose would be served? He believed he would be safe so long as he agreed to Jason's ultimatum.

Still, he couldn't help but wonder *Was it really over?*

A Note about the Author

Ronald D. Perkins is Professor Emeritus at a major university where he taught for thirty-two years and retired at the age of sixty five. He served as director of graduate studies for eight years and as chairman of his department for twelve years. He was actively involved in recruiting new faculty and participated in promotion and tenure decisions. *Tenure to Die For* is Dr. Perkins' second fictional story, the first entitled *Currents of Deceit: A Caribbean Eco-Thriller.*

Acknowledgements

I should like to express my gratitude to the following individuals for their suggestions and editorial assistance in preparation of this novel: Professor Emeritus S. Duncan Heron, Professor Emeritus Peter K. Haff, Dr. Alexander Glass, Norma Longo, and Edith L. Roberts. Technical assistance provided by Dr. Kyle J. Bradbury and Katheryne Doughty is also gratefully acknowledged.

The author is solely responsible for the content of this book and reiterates that it is purely fictional in content.